Twice a Princess

Twice a Princess

Susan Meier

THORNDIKE
CHIVERS

This Large Print edition is published by Thorndike Press®, Waterville, Maine USA and by BBC Audiobooks Ltd, Bath, England.

Published in 2005 in the U.S. by arrangement with Harlequin Books S.A.

Published in 2005 in the U.K. by arrangement with Harlequin Mills & Boon II B.V. 20033341

U.S. Hardcover 0-7862-7935-4 (Romance)
U.K. Hardcover 1-4056-3502-9 (Chivers Large Print)
U.K. Softcover 1-4056-3503-7 (Camden Large Print)

All characters in this book have no existence outside the imagination of the author and have no relation whatsoever to anyone bearing the same name or names. They are not even distantly inspired by any individual known or unknown to the author, and all incidents are pure invention.

The text of this Large Print edition is unabridged.
Other aspects of the book may vary from the original edition.

Set in 16 pt. Plantin by Christina S. Huff.

Printed in the United States on permanent paper.

British Library Cataloguing-in-Publication Data available

Library of Congress Cataloging-in-Publication Data

Meier, Susan.
    Twice a princess / by Susan Meier.
        p. cm. — (Thorndike Press large print romance)
    ISBN 0-7862-7935-4 (lg. print : hc : alk. paper)
    1. Large type books. I. Title. II. Thorndike Press large print romance series.
PS3563.E3463T87 2005
813'.6—dc22   2005014769

Special thanks and acknowledgment are given to Susan Meier for her contribution to the In a Fairy Tale World . . . series.

The Tale of the Cursed Princess

Not so very long ago there lived a princess with the reputation for being short-sighted, immature and spoiled rotten. Even her betrothed found her to be barely tolerable.

The princess's temper tantrums and selfishness eventually became too much for her family to bear. Her reaction to her father's marriage was the proverbial last straw. The king's only daughter loved being daddy's little girl, and the appearance of a potential stepmother threatened to change all that. The young princess tried to sabotage the engagement and the wedding. Her schemes were unsuccessful, but they convinced her godmother that the princess needed to be taught a lesson in humility and the power of love.

Her godmother cursed the princess with immediate advanced age, a severe bout of crankiness and exile from her country. The only way the princess could break the curse was to choose twenty-one potential couples and — using stories and a little magic —

bring love into their lives, a bond sanctified by marriage. Once the last marriage was performed, she would turn back into a princess and be welcomed home — as long as the last couple was joined before her thirtieth birthday.

If she failed to secure the marriages before time ran out, she would live in exile as a crone until her death. If she succeeded, however, she would return home to marry the prince she had been promised at birth, with a well-learned lesson of what it meant to truly love . . .

Chapter One

Nearly purring with joy over making her twenty-first love match, Princess Meredith Montrosa Bessart, known to the guests of La Torchere Resort as Merry Montrose, stood on the sidelines of the dance floor at the wedding reception of Cynthia Rawlings and Rick Barnett. Resplendent in his black tux, typically dark and brooding Rick gazed down at his beautiful blond bride as they glided along the dance floor, Cynthia's satin gown floating around them.

They looked like Cinderella and her prince, which to Merry was ironic considering that *she* was the real princess on Torchere Key, though a curse had changed her from a young, beautiful royal into a crone. Even dressed in her pretty blue gown, with her gray hair swept into a twist and wearing the diamond earrings and necklace — part of the collection of jewels belonging to Silestia's royal family that she'd been allowed to keep to remind her of home — she didn't look anything like a princess.

"Not dancing, Merry?"

The smooth baritone voice of Alexander Rochelle, owner of southwest Florida's La Torchere Resort and Spa, flowed over Merry from behind. Tingling with awareness, she took a second to compose herself before she turned around to face him.

Dressed in his black tux, his blond hair casually styled in sexy disarray and his blue eyes dancing, Alexander was so gorgeous, so tantalizing, that the breath in Merry's lungs disappeared, her chest tightened and her knees weakened. But the first fifteen seconds in Alexander's company were always like this. Not just because he was gorgeous, but because he had an air of excitement, power and sensuality about him that Merry hadn't seen matched. Not even in the court of Silestia, where her father was king.

He'd even had that air when he'd posed as a handyman.

"As resort manager I don't dance," she said slowly, forcing herself not to flirt with him. As a homely crone she would look ridiculous flirting with a handsome man. Though she had to admit that when she believed he was just a handyman, she had wanted to do more than flirt. He'd disguised himself to discover the secret of the resort's recent love matches, but he soon revealed himself as the resort's owner, first to her privately and then at a staff meeting. That same morning, he moved from a cramped employee efficiency apartment into the best villa on resort grounds, and he had been on La Torchere ever since, not really watching over her shoulder, but a hands-on owner to be sure. So, any thought she had of flirting had long ago died.

Still, that didn't mean she couldn't smile. Maybe even joke a little. "But if I did break protocol and dance at a guest's wedding, I certainly wouldn't do it in front of the boss."

Alexander laughed. Again, the smooth sound of his voice seemed to pour through Merry, touching her when she didn't want to be touched —

Well, that wasn't precisely true. She'd like nothing better than to be touched by this man. Tall and broad shouldered, with a deep and masculine voice that reminded her of dark liaisons and whispered secrets, Alexander Rochelle was so physically male that Merry couldn't imagine anything more feminine than being his lover. Just once in her life, she yearned to experience romance as intense, as perfect, as she was sure it would be with this man.

But she couldn't. Rick and Cynthia's marriage made their commitment official, finalizing the twenty-one matches that would break Merry's curse. She didn't know what would happen next. Literally! Right now, she stood before Alexander as a twenty-nine-year-old princess in a crone's body, but any minute now her physical appearance, regal bearing and comportment could be restored. Then Alexander Rochelle might be attracted to her, but it was her duty to return to Silestia to marry Prince Alec Montclair, the man to whom she had been promised.

That was one of the lessons she had learned during this curse. To respect and appreciate her life — including her duties. As a member of a royal family she had responsibilities. She was a leader, a ruler and one of the guards of the benevolent magic passed down through her lineage. She could be a tyrannical monarch — but because being a crone for seven years had shown her that being born a princess was a gift, not a curse — she had decided to fulfill her lot in life with joy.

And her lot in life was to marry Prince Alec.

"What if your boss — the actual owner of the resort for which you work — told you it was okay to dance?"

"Then I'd probably dance, but no one's asked me."

Alexander set his champagne glass on a convenient table and bowed elegantly before extending his hand to her. "Then allow me to ask you."

Tingles of attraction tiptoed through Merry, tempting her to place her fingers on his open palm and satisfy at least a little of her longing, and she gulped.

Being put under a curse and becoming old and haggard had been confusing, and it had taken her two years to adjust. Getting twenty-one couples together had been the struggle of a lifetime. The last five matches had been darned near impossible! She didn't want to blow her success because she was in lust.

Of course, who was to say dancing with Alexander would wreck her success? There was no way it could affect the twenty-one matches she had in place. Even if she tripped over his feet or drooled on his jacket, she couldn't embarrass herself because she hadn't yet transformed into Princess Meredith. No one at this resort even knew Princess Meredith existed. They knew Merry Montrose, resort manager, wrinkled-up old prune who looked about ten years past retirement, not three weeks away from her thirtieth birthday!

Damn it! It wouldn't hurt anything to

dance with Alexander, and certainly after seven long years of torture she deserved one tiny morsel of womanly joy.

Of course she did!

"I'd love to."

She placed her white-gloved fingers on Alexander's palm. Through the lace she could feel his warmth, his power. Pleasant shivers of excitement skipped up her arm. But when he slid his hand to the small of her back and nudged her as close to him as propriety allowed for a dance with an elderly woman, the shivers turned into a torrent of arousal. A very unacceptable torrent of arousal! After seven years of deprivation, being this close to a strong, sensual man nearly overwhelmed her. Heat shot through her and Merry honestly worried that she would faint.

"You've done a wonderful job with the resort."

Conversation! Thank God! She needed anything to get her mind away from the strength she could feel in his shoulders, the scent of his aftershave, the sensuality in his watchful eyes.

"Thank you."

"The fact that so many love matches seem to originate here hasn't hurt publicity."

Merry gulped again. "Thanks. I think."

He laughed. "Thanks is the appropriate

response. I was definitely complimenting you. La Torchere Resort is getting a reputation better than the fountain of youth. We're the fountain of love. If our number of guests continues to rise, we may have to add another wing to the hotel."

Merry held back a grimace. This time tomorrow she would be on her way home. The matchmaking would stop. The fountain of love wouldn't necessarily dry up, but it would surely slow down. "Don't send the project out to an architect yet."

"Why? Do you know something I don't know?"

"No," Merry hastily replied, probably too hastily, because he gazed down at her and Merry forgot everything but the latent fires of sensuality in his blue eyes. Standing so close, feeling his power as he effortlessly guided them around the dance floor, she was caught again in a yarn of yearning. What would it be like to kiss this man? To have him touch her and want her. . . .

"I think you *do* know something I don't know."

Jarred out of her thoughts, Merry said, "No." She paused to give him a reassuring smile and to remind herself that right at this moment she was a crone whom a man like Alexander wouldn't want on a lost bet. Also, with the curse broken, she would return to her true self, and as her true self she was promised to someone else. She had to stop fantasizing. "I don't."

"Okay." He smiled at her.

Merry's knees weakened again, and this time she couldn't seem to force them back to full strength. As she and Alexander floated along the dance floor, the lithe movements of his body brushing hers conjured all kinds of blissfully sensual images that would dissolve any woman. But Merry also remembered that with her curse broken she was probably experiencing the longings of a young woman because she was returning to her normal self. She didn't know how this curse worked, but there was a very real possibility that the blink of an eye could take her from crone to princess.

The blink of an eye?

Merry's heart bumped against her ribs. She really could zap back into a princess in the blink of an eye. After all, she'd become a crone in the time it took for her godmother to chant a few words. It wasn't impossible that she could suddenly find herself a princess in a crone's gown, having to explain the change to the man currently swirling her around the dance floor.

She had to get the heck away from Alexander Rochelle!

She drew a quick breath. "Alexander, I'm sorry," she said, bringing those soft blue eyes of his back to her again. "But I'm afraid I'm not feeling very well."

His features sharpened. "You're ill?"

His genuine concern touched a forgotten place in her heart. No one had cared about her for seven long years. But she wasn't sick and he wouldn't want to hear the real reason she needed to get away. So she fell back on her most obvious, and also most annoying, problem as a crone. "Maybe tired is a better word."

"You do look flushed."

Of course she did. Dancing with him had driven her to a state of excitement she hadn't felt in nearly a decade. It was a wonder she wasn't a puddle at his feet.

She smiled slowly, wearily, because acting was her ticket away from the temptation of his arms. "I'm simply tired. It's been a stressful week."

"Helping to plan a wedding hasn't made it any easier." Alexander stopped dancing, slid his arm from her waist and stepped back.

And Merry knew what Cinderella felt when she had to leave the ball. She could almost hear an imaginary clock striking midnight, as if announcing the end of something she wished could go on forever. But it couldn't. She stifled a powerful urge to weep and pulled her gloved hand out of Alexander's much larger one. As their fingers separated it seemed as if she were watching their destinies split, too. She belonged to someone else. They were not meant to be together.

Moving away from him, she sealed that fate. "Goodbye, Alexander."

But Alexander shook his head as he led her off the dance floor. "Oh, no. You're not walking to your quarters alone."

"I'm fine," Merry protested softly, though she knew she'd accept the assistance of whatever resort employee he pressed into service, if only to save an argument. She expected him to stop a passing waiter or to escort her to the bar where the bartender could ring the front desk. Instead he directed her to the ballroom entrance.

"What are you doing?"

"Walking you to your villa," Alexander calmly replied.

"You can't!" Panic skittered through her. Not only was she unbearably attracted to him and terrified she would make a fool of herself, but also she was changing. She was sure of it now. At any second she could zap back into a princess.

"I can."

"Alexander . . . Mr. Rochelle. You *can't*. You're one of the guests of honor at the wedding!"

"The bride and groom are the guests of honor." He guided her through the lobby, across the shiny green floor tiles, past the fountain that roared from a stone base to the skylight several stories above, to a glass double-door entrance in the back, which automatically opened.

When she didn't immediately step outside, he caught her arm to keep her moving and the heat of his hand on her flesh triggered responses that thundered through her. Her heart rate jumped to triple time.

"This isn't right!"

"This is fine." He urged her onto the garden path.

Moonlight spilled into the courtyard. The leaves of the palm trees swayed in the light breeze off the gulf. The Oasis pool waterfall shimmered in the distance. The scene couldn't have been more romantic if Merry had planned it herself, intensifying the continuing shivers of desire that trembled through her from his touch. Light-headed with fear, Merry picked up the pace.

★ ★ ★

When Merry Montrose began to walk faster, almost running to her cottage, Alexander Rochelle also quickened his steps. He wondered what she'd think if she realized she was being disrespectful to a monarch, then shoved that thought to the farthest corner of his brain. Being Prince Alec Rochelle Montclair wasn't merely stifling. It was a royal pain in the butt.

That was why he liked the United States. The people paid attention to royalty but money talked louder than titles and rich movie stars were of more interest to them. After Alec's betrothed, Princess Meredith Bessart, disappeared, he avoided the press by coming to the U.S., knowing that without money he really wasn't that amusing. But he soon realized that in a country as progressive as this one, he could reverse his family's financial misfortunes.

However, he also quickly saw that his business associates always assumed he had more money than he did because he was a prince, making deals difficult. So with a slight change of his first name and by dropping a few extra names he didn't really need, he became a commoner, someone expected to negotiate like a pit bull, and he built an empire.

In those seven years, his appearance had

also changed. He grew into his lanky frame, filled out, acquired a more mature demeanor and the stature of a man. People in his home country wouldn't even recognize him now, but, unfortunately, his good looks and newly acquired wealth had made him fodder for the paparazzi again.

He had come to La Torchere to check out the rumors about the many weddings that had recently taken place at his resort and eventually he decided to hide here. Not because he owned it, but because places such as this catered to people who didn't wish to be recognized or bothered. At La Torchere he had been comfortable, happy. And that was due in no small part to the woman beside him.

He stole a glance at Merry. She wasn't the most pleasant-looking female on the face of the earth. He guessed her age to be somewhere around sixty, but she appeared much older. Her gray hair was coarse and usually kept in a tight knot. Her nose had elongated with the passage of time. Her neck had enough folds that the necklace she wore could easily disappear and never be discovered again. But she was also the most interesting woman he'd met in a long time. He suspected there was a very good story behind her life.

Alexander had begun paying attention to her when he realized La Torchere's reputation as the fountain of love was due to Miss Merry's matchmaking. Oh, she was subtle. But as resort owner, Alexander noticed everything, and he knew this kooky old woman was the bottom line to his resort's most recent surge of success. He was even considering hiring an assistant for her to assure she could work for many more years.

"You should be back at the wedding reception."

Alexander shook his head. The wedding reception was the last place he wanted to be. He didn't like anything couched in pomp and circumstance. He'd had enough of it to last a lifetime when he was a child. His parents, a prince and princess of deposed monarchies in an arranged marriage, held ambassadorial roles that required them to represent their respective countries at so many functions that Alexander grew almost as tired of the pageantry as he did his parents' continued fighting. He'd believed arranged marriages were an archaic tradition that should be abolished until his father privately negotiated a trade agreement with the U.S., which his mother backed up with promises from her country. Then Alexander saw the purpose of their marriage. Silently, almost stealthily, a good ambassador could change a country's destiny.

With his current business acumen and knowledge of the United States, Alexander knew he probably didn't need an arranged marriage to change his country's destiny, but his betrothal to the princess from Silestia had opened trade routes he couldn't have opened on shrewdness alone. And he knew his country needed his marriage.

So he would do his duty when the time came. If and when Princess Meredith Bessart, the woman promised to him, came out of hiding, he would marry her and fulfill his princely responsibilities. Until then, he intended to pack as much living into these years of freedom as he possibly could. That meant he didn't go anywhere he didn't want to go.

"The wedding bored me." They reached the small stone path to her villa and Alexander directed her to turn, indicating that he would walk her to her door.

She sighed. "Really. I'm fine."

"And *I'm* fine. I never pass up the opportunity to take a moonlight stroll with a beautiful woman."

Merry laughed, but the sound came out as more of a cackle. Knowing she couldn't see him, Alexander winced at the horrible

23

sound. They reached the front door of her cottage and Merry stopped.

"I'm hardly a beautiful woman."

"Oh, I'd take exception to that," Alexander said, meaning it. He touched the spot where her heart beat beneath her thin gown and frail skin. "Here's where you're beautiful."

To Alexander's surprise, her eyes filled with tears and she blinked rapidly. "I'm not."

"You are."

"Alexander, get back to the party. Go find yourself a real beautiful woman because I think you're losing it."

He laughed. "Now that I'm sure you're okay, I will return to the party, but I don't need a beautiful woman."

She clicked her tongue. "Every man needs a beautiful woman."

From the look that came to her violet-blue eyes, he could see her matchmaker instincts kicking in. "Ah, ah, ah. It's not appropriate to play matchmaker for the boss."

Her cheeks reddened guiltily.

He laughed again. "Don't be embarrassed! Your matchmaking is a gold mine for the resort. I'm simply not interested."

Her gaze sharpened. "Not interested in *me* making you a match or not interested in any match at all?"

"Not interested in any match at all."

"You don't believe in love." She said it simply but sadly, and he lifted her chin to force her to look at him.

"A long time ago, in a kingdom far away," he began, speaking as if his life story were a fairy tale because he didn't want Merry to feel sorry for him. Princess Meredith's going into hiding had been a relief. The night of her coming-out ball, she had hurled insults that had devastated him, but they also taught him a good lesson. If and when he and Princess Meredith married, there would be no risk that he would lose his heart to her. He wanted to relate this tale so Merry saw the humor and the moral that he saw.

When she laughed her cackly giggle, Alexander knew she was on his wavelength and he continued, "I had a really bad experience."

"Someone hurt you?"

"Very much. But I also learned there was no such thing as love when I was young enough to put the lesson to good use, and I've protected myself." He paused, glancing at the thick, luscious foliage of the grounds before he added, "Placing your heart in someone's hands only gives them the power to hurt you."

"Really?" she asked softly, her voice so light and breathless, it sounded like the voice of a much younger woman. The change caused Prince Alec to look at her again but the moon had ducked behind a cloud and he really couldn't see her face in the shadows.

He smiled. "Yes."

"Your philosophy is sad, and makes your life sound lonely."

He shook his head. "Not at all. I might not believe in everlasting love, but I do whole-heartedly believe in romance."

She sighed with disgust. "You mean sex."

"No. I mean *romance*. Sweetheart notes. Flowers. Exciting trips. Carriage rides. Whispered secrets while tangled in satin sheets. Gifts. Stolen kisses." He smiled at her. *"Romance."*

Merry nearly swooned. Alexander Rochelle was adorable. Which made it doubly sad that his life was lonely. "You don't mind that your relationships end? I mean, aren't there problems?"

"Nothing that can't be solved with an honest conversation. Plus, before I start anything with a woman, I'm very open about expectations."

Confused because he didn't sound sad, or lonely, or even slightly bothered by his life choice, Merry asked, "And you like it that way?"

"I *love* it that way! Merry, I've courted

some of the most beautiful women in the world. I'm still friendly with most of them. Love doesn't have to be difficult. A person simply needs to understand when it's time to walk away."

Gazing at his handsome face, partially shadowed in the moonlight, Merry swallowed. That was another lesson she had learned from seven years as a matchmaker. Not every attraction ended in love. But that didn't make those liaisons wrong. People could enjoy a romantic short-term fling as long as both parties recognized when it was time to let go.

Given that circumstances in Alexander's life had hurt him enough to preclude him from taking the final step, which was complete trust, Merry had to concede that this life might be right for him. Because of knowing how and when to let go, he was a well adjusted, brilliant, romantic — yet realistic — man, and Merry suddenly wished with all her heart that she could have one of those temporary but romantic love affairs with him.

Because that wasn't a good idea for many, many reasons, she took a pace back. "You better return to the wedding."

He smiled softly. "Not before I kiss you good-night."

Merry's mouth fell open and she was absolutely positive her heart stopped. He couldn't want to kiss *her!* She was an obnoxious crone! Worse, her appearance could be changing even as they spoke. If he kissed her and realized she was young, how would she explain it?

She couldn't let him kiss her! It was insane!

She stepped back again, but he caught her gloved hand and lifted her fingers to his lips.

"Thank you, Merry, for doing such a wonderful job at the resort. I hope you will be with us for many, many years to come."

He let her fingers slide from his grip, turned and walked down the path again. A lone figure, bathed in moonlight, striding through the thick tropical foliage.

Tears filled Merry's eyes. He seemed well adjusted. He even exuded an air of sophisticated control. Yet, there was also an incompleteness about him. He might not want or even need a permanent relationship, but he'd never had a great love, and he never would because he would never trust the way he should.

Whether Alexander understood it or not, he was under as much of a curse as she was.

★ ★ ★

Merry's first thought when she woke the next morning was pure grief that she would never be romantic with Alexander Rochelle. She rubbed her eyes wearily, but she didn't feel the loose skin of her aged hand shift across her eyelids as it normally did. Instead, smooth, solid flesh greeted her.

Remembering that the lifelong commitment of Rick and Cynthia broke her curse and that she had begun to feel the changes to her appearance the night before, Merry shot up in bed. She looked down at her hands and saw slim fingers and barely lined palms. She flipped them over to reveal tight-skinned knuckles.

She tossed aside the covers and virtually flew to the mirror.

Dear God! She was tall again, shapely again, unwrinkled, unbent, tight-skinned, supple-muscled, auburn-haired and . . . gorgeous!

She was Princess Meredith Montrosa Bessart!

She could go *home!*

She could call her father! He would undoubtedly send a plane for her that day, and tomorrow morning she would wake up in her own bed. She could contact Prince Alec. . . .

And never see Alexander Rochelle again.

All her excitement faded and she drooped in front of the mirror as if she were still Merry Montrose. Damn it! Just when she had everything worked out, just when she had everything *figured out,* life threw the monkey wrench of Alexander Rochelle into the works.

She flopped onto her bed. Facing the glass double doors to the private patio of her villa, she saw the swaying palms of southwest Florida, and beyond the white sand, the blue waves of the Gulf, and her chest tightened.

Alexander.

The man simply made her heart hurt with longing. Prince Alec was her sworn duty, and never, ever would she consider shirking her responsibility. Never, ever would she make Alec feel that being his wife and partner was anything less than joy. She wanted to be Prince Alec's wife. She wanted to fulfill her roles.

But Alexander made her *yearn.* He made her long for things she'd never felt and never would feel because Prince Alec was not a love match. Though she was sure she would grow to love Alec, she didn't know if she would ever have romantic feelings for him, and because of the betrothal promise, he was her match for eternity.

She rose to pace. Eternity was a long time. She didn't want to spend eternity, or even the rest of her life, regretting that she'd never known romantic love. From observing the couples she had matched, she was also now wise enough to see that a person had to be ready for the love of honor, duty, responsibility and maturity. Her couples were lucky in that they seemed to combine both romantic love and the love of honor, but princesses weren't always that blessed. Her destiny wasn't that of a normal woman. Though she had to admit it seemed odd that fate had thrown Alexander in her path right when it was time to commit.

She paused by her bed. It *did* seem odd.

She began to pace again. In her seven years as matchmaker, she'd seen the roles of fate and magic in each union, and if there was one thing she had learned it was that fate didn't make mistakes or arrange anything without a purpose. Which meant Alexander had crossed her path at this precise point in her life for a reason.

A reason.

She paused again. Of course! It was so simple!

She was about to enter a life of duty and responsibility. And gladly. She wasn't merely being a good sport about this. She was committing with her heart and soul. And fate was rewarding her.

Or maybe fate was preparing her? If she truly was forfeiting romantic love, maybe fate was preparing her by gifting her with one season of romantic love? Something to fulfill her girlhood fantasies so she would be ready for her adult responsibilities.

That had to be it. There couldn't be any other explanation. Fate didn't torture. It didn't dangle something in front of a person to be cruel. Fate led, guided and rewarded.

Alexander Rochelle was her reward.

She had even wished for it the night before. When he walked her home and told her his theory of romance, she had wished to experience romance as intense as it would be with him.

She gasped when she realized fate had granted her plea, and her brain kicked into overdrive. To take advantage of this gift of fate, Merry had a lot of preparing to do. She was no longer the Merry the staff was expecting, but she was still the resort manager. She couldn't leave La Torchere in a lurch. In fact, she could probably prevent the fountain of love from disappearing and the number of guests from dwindling by hiring a replacement whom she could train to subtly slide the right people together. All she had to do was say she was Merry Montrose's niece and that her aunt had asked her to take over as resort manager for the time it took to find a replacement, so her aunt could retire.

It was so simple, so perfect, that Merry smiled. But her gaze collided with the cell phone on her bedside table and her smile turned to a look of confusion. As a crone, she'd used that magic cell phone to arrange everything from good weather to accidental meetings. She'd even had it repaired after a bout of frustration had left it in shambles.

Things would be a lot easier with Alexander Rochelle if . . .

No. It wouldn't be fair to manipulate Alexander with magic. . . .

That thought made her frown. Part of the reason it was a gift to be a Silestia royal was the magic she had at her disposal. And changing the weather to suit a picnic or arranging accidental meetings wasn't the same as hypnotizing Alexander or dousing him with love potion number nine. . . .

No. For some reason using her magic just didn't seem right. In fact, she was so sure it was inappropriate that she walked to the bedside table intending to stash the cell phone so she wouldn't be tempted, but the screen was blinking.

Don't waste your time,
Looking for a helpful rhyme.
No curse, no phone.
If you want love, find it on your own.

Well, that settled that. She didn't have access to the magic she'd been given as a crone, and she hadn't been fully schooled in her family's magic because she'd been a crone for most of the time she should have been at her father's knee, learning her family's legacy. But it didn't matter. She'd never needed magic to entice a man before.

She tossed the cell phone into the drawer of the bedside table and eyed herself critically in the full-length mirror.

Her first order of business was getting some decent clothes so she could go to the front desk and announce she was Merry Montrose's niece who was replacing her retiring aunt.

Her second was finding Alexander Rochelle and giving him the great romance of his life, becoming the woman *he* remembered forever.

Chapter Two

After a shower, Merry ran to La Torchere's boutique and purchased several outfits, which she instructed the staff to deliver to her villa. Then she scooted to the resort salon for a haircut, manicure and new makeup.

When she returned home, she found the three boxes from the boutique sitting on her bed and immediately shimmied into a formfitting teal suit. The color intensified the radiance of her auburn hair. Plus, the suit's fitted jacket and flirty short skirt were sexy enough that when she met Alexander to introduce herself as the replacement for her "Aunt Merry" she would make the impression she wanted to make.

By the time she finally strode up the cobblestone walk to the main lobby of the hotel, it was nearly noon. Her sleek, shoulder-length auburn hair had been styled to curve seductively around her face. A hint of mascara on her long black lashes accented her violet-blue eyes. Her lips were moist and dewy with her favorite lip gloss, and her pink-tipped toes peeked out of sexy white sandals.

It felt so good to be her real self that Merry could have wept. She would never take her youth, beauty or very lucky lot in life for granted again.

She stepped up to the glass double door of the lobby and it automatically opened. The roar of the three-story fountain in the center greeted her. Warm, honey-hued wood furniture with plump teal-and-cream-colored cushions surrounded a white baby grand piano. Lush tropical plants separated conversation areas.

Her heels tapped sensually on the shimmering forest-green tiles as she walked to the discrete front desk. Laying her perfect twenty-nine-year-old hand with brand new French nails on the golden oak counter, Merry said, "Hi. I'm Merry Montrose's niece."

Andi Jones, Merry's pride and joy, the clerk she had personally trained, smiled in welcome. Andi's navy skirt and white blouse were as crisp and professional as her polished manners. "Good afternoon, Ms. Montrose. I assume your aunt made reservations for you."

"Actually, no." Merry smiled briefly,

adopting the authoritative manner she'd perfected as Merry Montrose. "She hired me to take her place."

Andi's smile slipped, but didn't completely fade. "Excuse me?"

"Last night my aunt became ill at the wedding. Planning the reception exhausted her, so she called me. I arrived just before dawn to find her badly in need of a rest. She told me she wanted to retire, so I made arrangements for her to go home."

"I see."

"And I'm taking her place — at least long enough to find a real replacement for her. If anyone needs me, I'll be in my office."

"Yes, ma'am."

Merry almost turned away, but stopped herself. She wasn't Merry Montrose, the cursed crone who knew this resort like the back of her hand. She was supposed to be Merry's niece, a woman who had only arrived at the resort that morning.

She faced Andi again. "Could you show me to my office?"

Andi smiled politely and said, "Certainly, ma'am." But from behind Merry, Alexander Rochelle said, "Why don't you allow me?"

Merry's eyes widened. Darn it! Two minutes into her charade and she was already facing the ultimate test! Alexander Rochelle. As resort manager "Aunt Merry" might have had the power to hire her replacement, but Merry knew that as resort *owner* Alexander had final approval. She had hoped to establish herself with the staff before she "met" Alexander, so she would have the leverage of already being in place. Now she had nothing.

Still, if there was one thing she'd learned from her years as a matchmaker, it was that the best-laid plans could go astray. Fortunately, she had also learned she could handle anything life threw at her. She took a quick breath and faced Alexander.

As always, he was absolutely perfect. His light blue sport shirt complemented his pale blue eyes and blond hair. He left the first two buttons of the shirt open and might have appeared a bit too casual for his position as resort owner, but his creased khaki trousers and shiny brown loafers gave him the polish that kept his look sophisticated and professional.

Seeing him, Merry felt the air whoosh out of her lungs and for several seconds she couldn't speak. But that turned out to be very lucky because she had time to register that Alexander wasn't smiling at her, as he had been the night before when he walked "Aunt Merry" to her villa. He wasn't even smiling at her because she looked good in her teal suit and sexy white sandals. In fact, he appeared to be furious.

Either he was horribly upset that Merry Montrose had quit or he wasn't happy that "Aunt Merry" had hired her own replacement — and a niece no less. Princess Merry almost groaned at her stupidity. She should have realized Alexander Rochelle wouldn't take kindly to nepotism.

Alexander stared in amazement at the woman in front of him, unsure if he could contain his anger. After all these years, his betrothed, Princess Meredith Bessart, had the nerve to show up at his door. No announcement. No explanation. No warning. Just "Hello, I'm here to take over as manager of your resort."

As if he were going to let that happen!

Not about to let this woman make a fool of him as she had the night of her coming-out ball because he'd reacted from emotion, not logic, Alexander counted to one hundred, attempting to control his temper. But it was no use. He was livid. How dare she just stroll in and take over his resort!

"I'm sorry," Princess Meredith said,

smiling brightly as she extended her hand to him in the standard American greeting. "But I didn't get your name."

Alexander's eyes narrowed. *She didn't know him?*

Actually, that *was* possible. He'd been as far underground as she had been for the past seven years. There weren't pictures documenting his growth from a gangly twenty-four-year-old to the seasoned thirty-one-year-old he was now. Anyone who hadn't seen him in seven years wouldn't connect the tall, spindly boy to the broad-shouldered, confident man he was today.

Alexander smiled. Once again, the combination of his maturing appearance and his slightly changed name had hidden his identity.

And for the first time in his acquaintance with pampered Princess Meredith, he had the upper hand.

"I'm Alexander Rochelle," he said as he took the hand she had extended, playing along because he was about to zap her and he was going to enjoy it. "What did you say your name was?"

"I'm also Merry Montrose. I'm the namesake of my aunt."

"Well, Merry Montrose, I own this resort. And though your aunt Merry certainly did have the power to hire her replacement, you must be approved by me."

Merry said, "I understand."

She understood? Her agreement astounded Alexander so much he almost took a pace back. Since when did Princess Merry accept a situation she didn't like?

Maybe she hadn't gotten the full message.

"Not only do I have the power to reject her choice, but in this case I'm not sure I agree with her decision."

Her expression became grave. "Again, I understand. This is all coming out of the blue for you. But my aunt didn't hire me to take her place permanently. I'm here to find her replacement." She caught his gaze and smiled prettily. "So she doesn't feel horrible for leaving you without warning."

Alexander swallowed as unwanted sexual awareness snaked through him. Princess Meredith had one powerful smile. His betrothed might be a spoiled brat, but she was a *gorgeous* spoiled brat. Shiny auburn hair framed her face and set off the unusual violet hue of her eyes. Her full, glossy lips begged to be kissed. The suit she wore showcased her absolutely perfect figure. Any man would find her attractive.

Luckily, he'd learned his lesson about

falling under the spell of her beauty. He took a step back, away from her.

Princess Meredith continued, "My aunt told me so much about your resort that I'm probably the best person to find someone to replace her. From the minute she began her work here, I knew her every move," she said with a light laugh, cajoling him, flirting with him, again shooting sexual responses through his veins, tempting him to flirt back.

Determined not to let her get to him, Alexander didn't answer right away. He didn't understand why Princess Meredith wished to perform the menial task of replacing her aunt, but he also realized he wasn't handling the situation properly. As owner of the resort, he shouldn't be wondering why Princess Merry was here. His real concern should be that he'd lost his perfect manager. And without explanation. He and Merry Montrose were close enough that she wouldn't have left without telling him.

"I walked your aunt to her villa last night and she never mentioned retiring."

"She didn't realize how tired she was until she awakened this morning." Princess Merry smiled brightly. "I think she would have worked here forever if things hadn't . . . changed . . . last night."

Alexander honed in on the mistake.

42

"Something changed? I thought you said she was merely tired?"

"Tired enough to retire," Princess Meredith assured him. "She'd never been quite that tired before."

Alexander crossed his arms on his chest as Princess Meredith stood smiling at him, waiting for his verdict. He'd known Merry Montrose was tired, but he also knew she was proud of the job she'd done at La Torchere and he didn't believe she was the type of person to retire. More than that, though, as the owner of a resort, he was quite familiar with the power of a good vacation. Even if Merry were exhausted enough to *think* she needed to retire, he genuinely believed that once his very active manager got two weeks of peace and privacy she would be bored. And he had to wonder if she hadn't sent her spoiled niece, a woman with no experience at all, because she was trying to hold her job for herself without looking obvious.

That made a great deal of sense.

Princess Meredith being chosen as a temporary replacement also meant there was a good possibility Alexander would get his wonderful manager back. All he had to do was work with Princess Meredith for about two weeks.

He studied her delicate features, her pretty eyes, her serene smile. Whether those weeks would be two *loooong* weeks or two short weeks would be determined by the behavior of his betrothed. Merry Montrose might not have known she was sending her niece to work for her future husband, but Alexander knew. And he wasn't sure he could work with his spoiled, selfish fiancée long enough for Merry Montrose to realize she wanted her old job back.

The phone rang and, jarred out of his thoughts, Alexander noticed he and Merry had attracted a crowd of curious staff who milled around the lobby desk pretending to be busy. If he didn't make a decision quickly, he and Merry would undoubtedly be the topic of conversation at lunch today.

He glanced at his betrothed with her sexy little suit, her soft violet eyes and her shiny auburn hair that caught the sunlight pouring in from the skylight above the fountain. The only real weapon she had was sex appeal, and it would be a cold, frosty day in hell when he let sex appeal affect the way he ran his business or distract him from doing what he needed to do.

"Let's talk in your aunt's office," he said, directing Princess Meredith to a corridor to the right. Without waiting for her, he walked away.

Because he kept his gait deliberately long, Merry scrambled to keep up with him. "I'm sorry Aunt Merry quit without giving notice."

He frowned. Since when did Princess Meredith know about notices? "Don't worry about it. I realized myself that she was tired."

"Then you understand?"

Actually, he probably understood a lot better than Princess Meredith did. Right now Merry Montrose needed rest, and the only way Alexander could assure she would return would be if he kept Meredith here so Merry Montrose would know her job was still open.

He wasn't thrilled with the situation, but he *did* have the upper hand, so he wasn't worried. "Yes. I understand."

They reached the doorway to Merry's office, but rather than go inside, he stopped.

"You can stay."

"You won't be sorry!" Merry said and just barely stifled the urge to throw her arms around him and kiss him soundly. But before she had a chance, Alexander Rochelle pivoted and was halfway down the hall to the lobby.

Merry sighed. This was not working out the way she had hoped. She'd seen the flares of sexual awareness that flamed in Alexander's eyes but he'd quickly banked them as if he didn't want to be attracted to her.

Stepping into her office and walking across the charming blue-and-white braided rugs that sat atop the hardwood floors, Merry considered that maybe Alexander had tempered his reaction to her because he didn't get personally involved with employees. After all, she'd never seen him "date" a member of the staff. She decided that would be a reasonable, but conquerable, problem — except, having any kind of difficulty to overcome took away precious time. She would have to think of something spectacular to force him to get beyond his reservations quickly.

In fact, now that she had explained crone Merry Montrose's disappearance and had herself established as the resort manager, the next order of business was calling her father to see how much time she did have.

She fell to the slate-blue leather chair behind the honey-colored desk, lifted the receiver of the cordless phone and dialed his private number. She waited three rings before his manservant answered.

"Charles! Charles! It's Princess Merry!

46

My goodness! It's so good to hear your voice."

Dead silence greeted her and Merry frowned. She supposed she should expect this kind of reaction. Not only had she been out of touch for seven years, but also she hadn't exactly been the kindest princess in the world.

"I'm sorry I didn't get the chance to say goodbye before I left, Charles."

Again silence.

Her frown deepened but Merry decided to save her fence-mending for when she got home. "Is my father around?"

"Yes, Mum."

"Great. May I speak with him, please?"

"Yes, Mum."

She waited only two seconds before her father was on the line.

"Merry! My God! Where the hell have you been? Are you okay? The only contact we've had were those notes you sent through Lissa!" he said, referring to the godmother who had cursed her. "We understood you wanted an American education, but did you really need to go to school disguised as a commoner?"

Merry swallowed a giggle. She'd wondered how Lissa had explained the curse to her father. Since it was all over now, and because she had learned valuable lessons, she wouldn't argue Lissa's convenient story and said simply, "Yes. My classes are done now."

"I'll send a plane."

"No, Dad, I can't come home today." She needed to find a real replacement for herself to fulfill her responsibility to the resort, but more than that she wanted her reward time with Alexander. "I won't be home for two weeks."

"Two weeks?"

"Yes," she said, strolling away from her desk and walking to the mirror in her private powder room where she smiled contentedly at her reflection. "I want a few weeks to adjust to being myself."

"Adjust to being yourself?"

Merry grimaced at her slip, but she also realized that she'd just revealed a tidbit of information about her curse and it had come out as real words, not gibberish. Up to this point, every time she'd tried to explain her curse, she couldn't. She couldn't even give tiny details. With the curse broken, she could explain the real story to her dad.

"Merry?"

She drew a quick breath. In spite of the fact that Lissa had created an acceptable excuse for her disappearance, Merry wanted to tell her father the truth. She wanted him

48

to understand her hardships and to see there was a good reason she'd changed so much, so he would understand that she wouldn't revert to being a spoiled princess.

Still, this wasn't a story one told over the phone. This was a story a daughter told in private, in her father's study, sipping cocoa, when she could be herself. Not a member of a royal family, but a daughter. "I'll explain everything when I get home."

She could hear the warning in her father's voice when he said, "I'm counting on it."

"Dad, really. I haven't done anything wrong, or foolish, or frivolous. How about this? I promise to be home for my birthday."

He sighed. "That's *three* weeks!"

Considering that this was all the time she'd have with Alexander to satisfy the yearning of her soul for one great love, Merry's heart dipped. Her voice was filled with sadness when she said, "Three weeks isn't such a long time."

Apparently picking up on her melancholy, her father relented and softly said, "I suppose."

"Thanks, Dad." Tears pricked Merry's eyes. Though he was a king, her father always deferred to her, always loved her — even when she'd made his life miserable for remarrying after her mother's death. Lord, she'd been absolutely horrid!

Regret swamped her and she squeezed her eyes shut. She had a lot to make up for when she returned home. "I love you, Dad."

From her dad's quickly indrawn breath, she knew she'd surprised him. After a moment of silence, he whispered, "I love you, too."

Merry tried all afternoon to think of something spectacular that would push Alexander into breaking or bending any rules he might have about getting involved with a co-worker, but she couldn't think of anything. It wasn't until she walked past the window of La Torchere Boutique at the end of the day and saw a white thong bikini that a plan formed.

If anything could render a man incapable of resisting a woman, it would be that suit. And as the resort manager, who had insider knowledge of Alexander's activities, Merry knew the perfect way to be alone with him when he saw her in it. Every night Alexander had a drink beside his private pool before he ordered dinner from the Green- house Café. All she had to do was pretend to be lost and walk in on him and voilà. . . . She'd render him speechless. After a little flirting — to prove she was interested in him and to let him know he didn't have to worry about her telling tales to the staff — he'd be helpless.

Her plan was perfect.

Merry strode into the boutique and ten minutes later marched out with her secret weapon. But she wasn't quite so confident when she slid into the skimpy white bikini and eyed herself critically in the full-length mirror of her bedroom.

The scant material barely covered the appropriate areas, but she didn't think the suit's skimpiness was the problem. Her hips and thighs were trim and toned. Her tummy was flat. Her breasts were firm. She'd worn this kind of suit a million times before she'd been cursed. So why did something not feel right? And why was that "something" making her stomach churn?

Deciding her odd feeling could simply be nervousness about her night with Alexander, Merry slipped on her blue-violet crocheted cover-up and sneaked out of her villa in the dying light. Wavy clouds of red, pink and aqua applauded the sun for its hard day of work as it made its final descent. Soon it would be dark and she would be in Alexander's arms. Excitement quivered through her at all the wonderful possibilities that awaited her. But imagining being kissed and held and loved by Alexander also caused Merry's queasiness to return.

She stopped on the cobblestone path when she reached the fork that gave visitors the option of walking to the beach or turning toward Alexander's residence. She glanced toward his villa. Though he was owner of La Torchere, Alexander hadn't wanted his quarters to stand out in any way, so in terms of size and shape, his cottage looked the same as all the others. An open cobblestone path was surrounded on both sides by the resort's trademark foliage. But that plant life also camouflaged the biggest difference between his villa and the others — a fence that surrounded a private pool.

She knew the gate would be open because every night the guards reported locking it for him. She knew his habits. She had the opportunity. And she looked great. Besides, she didn't have enough time to wait for him to notice her. At most, she had three weeks before she had to go home. She had to start something tonight.

Anticipation trembled through her as she slid through the gate. Covertly peeking through the sliding glass door to his living room, Merry could see his black leather sofa in the muted glow of a single lamp, the light a fairly clear indicator that he was home.

Nervous, she slid out of her cover-up. She couldn't decide if she should be in the pool or be lying on a chaise when he came out with his drink. Then she realized a splash from her dive into the water would conveniently alert him that he had a visitor. Time wasn't her friend. She had to get things moving as quickly as possible. She draped her cover-up over the chaise and dived into the pool. By the time she came up for air, Alexander was opening his sliding glass door.

"What the . . . *Merry?*"

Her heart skipped a beat at the sight of him. That afternoon, he had changed out of his typical resort attire and into a black suit for a meeting, and right now, with the jacket removed and the sleeves of his white shirt rolled to his elbows, he looked sexily rumpled.

Though it was difficult, Merry managed to sound composed when she said, "Oh, hello, Alexander. What are you doing here?"

"I *live* here."

She glanced around as if confused. "We all live here."

"No, I live *here*," he said, pointing at the ground beneath his feet. "This is my villa and that," he said, pointing again, "is my private pool."

"Private pool?" She feigned a gasp, pretending she didn't know he had a private pool since this was her "first day" as manager, and hoisted herself up on the ladder. Water sensuously trickled from her hair to her shoulders, from her shoulders to her breasts, from her breasts down her flat-as-a-pancake stomach to the string that perched on her hip bones. She shook her hair off her face and tucked it behind her ears. "What do you mean, private pool?"

"This is my villa. This is my pool," he said, slowly, because he couldn't stop his eyes from taking in the scenery she provided. As he looked at her, she watched his pale irises heat to a blue flame, confirmation of what she believed she had seen that afternoon. He found her as attractive as she found him.

Shivering with a combination of nervousness and her own desire, Merry swallowed hard before she said, "My villa doesn't have a pool."

"*You*," he reminded her, raising his gaze away from her taut body until it angled with hers, "are the help." She could tell from his tone that he was trying very hard to remain righteously indignant, but nothing he said dimmed the fire in his eyes. "I'm the owner. I get one of the deluxe villas. You get a darned good one, but not deluxe."

From the tone of his voice, it was clear he wanted to be furious with her, but the way his gaze continually fell to her body proved other emotions warred with his anger. Still, that was a good sign. A battle had to be fought and won. His eyes were supposed to stray to her body. His feet were supposed to remain rooted to the spot, as if he couldn't turn away. He was supposed to try to walk away and fail. He was doing exactly what needed to be done.

So why didn't she feel triumphant?

Watching his gaze fall again to her breasts, Merry suddenly knew why she didn't feel any sense of victory. This was a purely sexual encounter. Even her own responses were physical, not emotional. But theirs was supposed to be a romantic relationship. A time of great love that they both could remember forever. And right now there was nothing romantic about the way he was looking at her.

She stepped in front of him, not so close as to be inappropriate, but near enough that he was forced to look at her face. In a deliberate effort to shift the mood, she softly said, "I'm sorry. I didn't mean to intrude on your privacy."

He drew a long breath and quickly averted his eyes, but not before she saw the look of discomfiture in them. And she knew why everything had gone awry. Being with a nearly naked stranger embarrassed him.

"Just get back to your own quarters."

With that he turned and all but ran to his sliding glass door, which he closed so hard the glass rattled. Then he snapped the vertical blind closed.

Merry blinked rapidly. Her hope melted into the realization that she hadn't just failed, she'd embarrassed Alexander enough that he might never speak to her again.

She grabbed her cover-up, then turned and scrambled away from his villa, before anyone could see she'd been in the boss's private quarters. But her steps slowed as the soothing sounds of the night calmed her. The *whoosh-whoosh-whoosh* of the waves lulled her into thinking clearly, and she began to understand not just Alexander's reaction but why she'd had her own odd feeling about her plan right from the start.

It wasn't the suit. The suit was merely a symptom of her bigger misjudgment. Seven long years had passed since she'd been flirty Princess Merry. The tricks she'd used to entice men didn't work anymore . . . or maybe those tricks didn't work with mature men.

Alexander was certainly a mature man. That was part of the attraction. She didn't want to have the romance of her life with a silly boy. She wanted a man. And a man didn't respond to a girl's tricks.

And now he would be wary of her. She had three short weeks to share a romance with him and she'd put him so much on the defensive that she would probably spend most of that time convincing him she was harmless.

That is, if he stayed in the same room long enough for her to speak to him again!

She'd blown it.

Chapter Three

After the blind on his sliding glass door closed with a satisfying snap, Alexander turned and marched across the corner of the Oriental rug that sat beneath the black leather sofa and matching chair of his living room. Without stopping, he strode through the dining room, which was furnished with only a long oak table and ladderback chairs arranged atop a bright red area rug on sand-colored ceramic tile, and bounded into the galley kitchen he never used.

He didn't know what the devil was going on with Princess Meredith Bessart, but from her behavior by his pool it was abundantly clear that the woman who had once told him she found him repulsive had just thrown herself at him.

He knew he'd matured in the past seven years. He wasn't the ugly duckling prince she had insulted at her coming-out ball. So it wasn't inappropriate to assume that she might not find him repulsive anymore. He'd also grown accustomed to women hitting on him. Most wanted his money. The few in Europe who knew his real identity wanted a piece of his royal stature. But Princess Meredith had her own money. She had her own royal position. He didn't have anything she might want. Her making a pass at him didn't make any sense.

That was why he tossed his hardly touched Scotch into the sink and rinsed it down the drain with a quick splash from the faucet. He needed a clear head to think this through. The princess had almost bested him out there by his pool. Not because he couldn't resist her, but because he hadn't realized he'd *have to* resist her. He assumed that while she was here, she'd play at resort manager, boss around the staff and flirt with the guests. He hadn't expected her to flirt with *him*. Caught off guard as he had been, every male instinct he possessed had burst to life.

And why not? Spoiled or not, selfish or not, Princess Meredith was one gorgeous, sexy woman. A cloistered monk would have trouble resisting her.

Of course, the easy answer to this dilemma was never to be in the position of having to resist her again. All he had to do was stay away from her. If she were here looking for fun and she'd decided to make chasing him the sport of the day, his avoiding her actually suited two purposes. He would not only save himself from her flirting, but also Aunt Merry might return more quickly when the princess got bored and called her aunt to complain. It was such a clever yet uncomplicated plan that Alexander relaxed.

He easily ignored her for two whole days. Until Princess Meredith called a meeting of the executive staff that Alexander couldn't miss. But given that all department heads were required to attend, he wasn't worried.

Unfortunately, when he arrived at the first-floor conference room before anyone else and found himself alone with his betrothed, he stopped dead in his tracks.

Dressed in a very covering apricot-colored suit and strappy brown sandals, Princess Meredith wasn't intending to be sexy, but she was nonetheless. Her suit jacket and little skirt fit her as if both were made to accent the attributes of her perfect figure. But more than that, she couldn't hide her sensual red-brown hair or her bedroom eyes.

Still, Alexander didn't panic. He said good morning and took his seat at the far end of the table — giving Merry the place at the head, the same as he had with her aunt

— and diverted his attention to the meeting handouts.

After only a cursory review of the week's registry, which reported that three single men and two single women had opted out of the final two days of their resort stays, Alexander's entire demeanor changed, and he forgot all about Merry's curves. With a pampered princess at the helm of his resort for only three days, the business was in trouble. Left to her own devices, she was tanking his resort!

The time for ignoring Princess Meredith was over. He wanted Merry Montrose back. Now.

Without looking up from the spreadsheet, Alexander said, "The early departure figures are distressing."

Merry cleared her throat. "Well, sometimes little things like this happen in a transition."

"*Little things?*" Alexander asked, leaning back in his seat. "Five guests left early." He caught her gaze. "That means they were bored."

"I'll tell Constance, the activities director, to step up her efforts to get the men and women involved in games or sports together." Clearly nervous, Merry rose to get a cup of coffee.

"I don't think so," Alexander began, but his attention was unexpectedly snagged by the way the soft material of her skirt rounded the curve of her bottom and a vivid image of that same bottom in the thong bikini wound through his brain.

His mouth watered.

Disgusted with himself for being weak, Alexander immediately shifted his eyes upward. Unfortunately Princess Meredith simultaneously turned away from the coffeepot to face him. His gaze fell on the V created by her buttoned jacket, and he found himself staring at her cleavage.

Angry that his thoughts kept veering in the wrong direction, and more eager than ever to get his real manager back, he tossed the spreadsheet across the shiny conference-room table and sharpened his tone.

"Your aunt Merry handled things like this personally! And I want these numbers to go back to the way they were when *she* ran things." He paused and caught the princess's gaze. "I was with her the night before she left. She was tired. That's all. She didn't talk of retiring. She most certainly didn't talk about replacing herself and I'm not at all happy with your being here."

Princess Merry drew a quick breath, but before she could answer him, the conference-room door opened and head concierge Lissa Piers entered. A middle-aged woman with brown hair that was almost always pulled into a tight bun, Lissa wore the navy skirt and white shirt of the hotel lobby employees. A big smile lit her beatific face until she saw Alexander. Then her smile faded like the rays of the sun covered by a cloud. She glanced from Alexander to Merry, then back to Alexander again.

Her face reddened guiltily and Alexander suddenly remembered something that had been right under his nose all along. Merry Montrose, Princess Meredith's aunt, may not have known he was Prince Alec, but Lissa Piers *did* and Lissa was Princess Meredith's godmother. With Princess Meredith acting as if she were totally unaware of his real identity and with Lissa's face currently as red as two tomatoes, it made sense to consider that Lissa — not Princess Meredith — was behind his betrothed's sudden appearance at his resort.

Well, he would put a stop to any plan Lissa had right now.

"Come in, Lissa," he said, his voice as smooth and dangerous as good Kentucky whiskey.

Lissa took a shaky step into the room. She said, "Good morning, Merry." But her gaze was on Alexander, her eyes wide and bright. She knew she was in trouble.

Oblivious to the tension between Alexander and Lissa, Merry said, "Alexander, I don't know if Lissa told you this, but she's my aunt and my godmother."

Lissa's eyebrows rose in surprise, as if she hadn't expected Merry's revelation.

Alexander's eyes narrowed. That introduction basically confirmed that Princess Meredith really didn't know who he was. Otherwise, she wouldn't have introduced him to a godmother he had already met.

Still, he couldn't understand why Merry thought it relevant to mention she and Lissa were related until Merry added, "I hope you don't have a problem with relatives working together."

Then he understood. He had been short with Princess Meredith from the minute she showed up at the resort, even before she appeared at his pool, so she assumed he was angry because her aunt Merry had hired a relative to be her temporary replacement. That assessment wasn't just wrong, it also caused a major problem for Alexander. If Merry Montrose thought Alexander was angry with her for hiring her niece, she could fear returning.

"No," he said, intending to nip that misconception in the bud. "As long as everyone does his or her job, I don't care who they're related to."

Merry said, "Good." Then she faced Lissa, who had taken a seat. "Lissa, when you arrived, Alexander and I were talking about my Aunt Merry's retirement and I was about to remind him that I'm only here temporarily."

Surprised because he thought Merry would have been glad for the distraction of Lissa's entrance to take them away from that topic, Alexander said, "Yes, I remember."

"When I took my aunt's place three days ago, I told my dad I'd be here three weeks," Merry continued. "I have to confess that for the past two days I've been considering leaving early, but then I saw the departure numbers and I realized I couldn't. I intend to stay until I get those numbers where they should be. Neither my aunt nor I want to see the resort suffer because she retired."

Alexander stared at her. From the way she talked, it was clear that she honestly thought she could fix this problem. Worse, she genuinely thought he wanted *her* — the princess who hadn't worked a day in her life — to stay!

"But I've already lost three days of my

three weeks and I can't extend it. My father is insisting I return home on my thirtieth birthday." She drew a quick breath. "And I have to abide by his wishes because I have a commitment."

"And it's a *big* commitment, Mr. Rochelle," Lissa said, snagging his attention and his gaze.

From the expression in Lissa's eyes, he could see she expected him to get some kind of meaning from what Merry had said. He frowned. Merry couldn't stay because she had to return home to fulfill a commitment.

The only commitment of hers that he knew about was . . .

Oh, Lord.

She was returning home to marry him! This time next month he could be married to her!

When the meeting ended, Alexander grabbed Lissa's arm and, careful to keep his grip dignified but firm, he guided her to the back exit of the lobby, down the cobblestone path and to his villa. He didn't say a word until they were behind the closed door, then he turned on her.

"What in the hell is going on?"

Lissa smiled. "I'm not entirely sure myself."

"Oh, come on! I know who you are! I

know who *she* is!" Alexander headed for his bar, but changed his mind and faced Lissa again. "I'm not so naive that I don't recognize that she's here for a reason! And whatever it is, you're in on it."

Lissa shook her head. "Princess Meredith is only my niece. She's not obligated to tell me her plans."

"So she has a plan?"

"I have no idea," Lissa said with a laugh. "But if I were to guess, I'd say she's taking something of a vacation before she goes home to face her father."

Alexander had assumed Merry was going home to announce she would be keeping her commitment to marry him, so Lissa's reply surprised him. "What do you mean, face her father?"

"Do you think you're the only person who hasn't seen her in seven years?"

"Yes. I thought she was hiding from me. Trying to get out of our marriage."

"Not exactly, but I'm really not at liberty to tell you that story. When the time is right, Princess Meredith will tell you."

"Frankly, I don't give a damn about why she left. But I do give a damn about what's going to happen when she goes home."

Not hedging or playing coy, Lissa bluntly said, "You don't want to marry her?"

"I'm *honor-bound* to marry her."

"And I can see it thrills you to pieces."

He sighed. He had no intention of explaining to Lissa that only a fool would be "thrilled" by a marriage that was at best a negotiation at worst a war. His parents' arranged marriage had shown him there was no room for sentiment in a union brought about for the purposes of nations.

"It doesn't matter if I'm thrilled or not."

Lissa's voice softened. "Of course it does. Do you think I want my goddaughter in an unhappy marriage?"

"I think neither Merry nor I has much choice."

"You could petition to get out of the arrangement."

He shook his head. "No, I can't. Merry might have made a promise to her father, but I made a pledge to my *country*."

"Then it looks like you'll have to get her to break the engagement since hers is the lesser of the two promises."

"I don't want her to break the commitment. My country needs this alliance."

"Then you're more stuck than you think. Because your country needs this alliance, and I don't want my godchild unhappily married, you need to figure out a way to make this marriage happy."

Alexander shook his head as if amused. "Arranged marriages aren't supposed to be happy. In our case, there's even less chance."

"Why?"

"Because your godchild is a selfish spoiled brat."

Lissa unexpectedly brightened. "Not anymore. Seven years away have completely changed Princess Meredith."

He eyed her skeptically. "I doubt it."

"Oh, Alexander, you don't have to believe me. All you have to do is spend some time with her and you'll see that she's not the princess who stormed out on everyone seven years ago."

Alexander snorted. "As if she'd be honest in front of me."

"From what I saw at that meeting, she's very honest with you."

"You mean she's honest in front of *her boss*."

"And you are her boss. So she's honest with *you*."

He frowned and fell to his black leather chair. Though it was true that Princess Merry had treated him with an honesty of sorts, it was also true that she'd thrown herself at him a few days ago by the pool. Of course, he wasn't about to tell Lissa that. "This is preposterous."

"Not really." Lissa sat on the corner of the sofa beside Alexander's chair and placed her hand on his forearm. "You have an opportunity with your betrothed that most couples in arranged marriages don't have. The chance to get to know each other without your impending marriage hanging over your heads. Princess Merry doesn't have a clue who you are. If you play your cards right for the next two and a half weeks, not only can you see her real personality, but also you can show her *your* real self."

"I don't want any part of a charade."

"Unless you and Merry strike some kind of deal right now, the rest of your life is going to be a charade. At state dinners and royal events, you're going to have to pretend to like her." Lissa paused, then smiled at Alexander. "Why not see if you really do like her?"

"I don't."

"She's changed."

"No one can change that much."

Lissa slapped both of her hands on her knees, then rose. "Merry has. And you have a chance to let her prove it to you, even as you prove to her that you're not the backward young prince she left behind seven years ago." She walked to the door. "Your choice. Call her into your office today, lay your cards on the table and have the stiff, impersonal marriage you seem to think is your destiny. Or give her a chance to show you she's different." She smiled at him. "Better yet, give yourself a chance to show her *you're* different. You're not the boy she pushed around at her coming-out ball, Prince Alec," she said, using his royal name and shoving him into the role of monarch whether he wanted to be there or not. "Maybe she needs a chance to see that for herself."

Lissa left and Alexander sighed heavily. He didn't like games. But Lissa had a point. He might not think it worth his time to give Merry an opportunity to prove she'd changed, but there was merit to showing his betrothed that he wasn't the pushover she'd left behind. He was the director of an empire, and she didn't have a clue what she would be getting into when she married him. Forget about his newfound wealth. Forget about his better looks. He was now a man of confidence and power. A man who could best her in a fight because he could bring his own power to bear against her family's throne. They weren't unevenly matched anymore.

He supposed it would save everybody time and theatrics if Princess Meredith saw his new station in life as an objective observer rather than as his betrothed — or his wife. Because he intended to marry her. His country needed this alliance.

Standing by the door of her villa at ten minutes past midnight, Merry glanced at her white lace cover-up, but decided against taking it. She opened the door and stepped out into the warm night, heading up the cobblestone path to the Oasis pool. She wore a brand new "tankini" that she'd bought when she tossed her thong bikini into the trash. The sexy bottoms were cut high, and the accompanying top met their waist. It was sexy, but still respectable.

The suit was the perfect attire for a resort manager to wear when she joined the guests who couldn't sleep. Tonight Merry planned to mingle and hopefully put a single person or two together to prevent any more guests from checking out early. If it killed her, she would show Alexander she could do the job while she looked for a permanent replacement. She no longer planned to seduce him. The man didn't like her. He was *attracted* to her. He found her pretty and sexy and might even want to sleep with her. But he wasn't going to do anything about it because he didn't like her — and she knew why.

From a few slipped sentences in their argument before the staff meeting that morning, she realized he believed she had taken her "Aunt Merry" away from him and was now keeping her away. In a sense, he was correct. Because she couldn't turn into a crone again, she couldn't bring Merry Montrose back to La Torchere. But Alexander liked the efficient old crone. He liked the job she had done for him. And he wanted her to work for him again.

Which was sweet, but made Princess Meredith's situation impossible. She couldn't explain that there was no Aunt Merry. She would have to get him to accept a replacement. But without her matchmaking magic, she couldn't seem to do the job of resort Cupid that she'd done as a cursed crone. Unwittingly, she was giving him the impression only Merry Montrose could manage this resort.

When she reached the Oasis patio, moonlight glistened off the water of the Olympic-size pool. The sound of the waterfall hummed around her. Lush tropical gardens welcomed her. Unfortunately, there wasn't a guest in sight.

"All by yourself?"

Hearing Alexander Rochelle's voice, Merry spun around. Standing on the edge of a cluster of palm trees and hibiscus, he was partially hidden by shadows created when moonlight hit the palms. But his masculine voice was enough to send a shiver of feminine pleasure through her. She had no idea why he'd chosen to swim in one of the public pools when he had a private pool, but she wasn't about to say anything that might remind him of her embarrassing failed seduction of a few nights ago.

"I had hoped I wouldn't be. This was one of my best places for matchmaking."

"One of *your* best places?"

She barely stopped a gasp at her own stupidity. That was a slip she shouldn't have made. "I meant my aunt Merry's. She told me she introduced a lot of couples here. I was hoping to do the same, so no one else checked out early."

"Oh," he said, stepping out of the shadows and into the moonlight. Soft-looking tufts of pale hair covered his chest. His arms were well shaped and muscular. Black swim trunks, like boxers, revealed tanned thighs. His feet were bare. "It seems your plan failed. It's just you and me tonight."

The sensual timbre of Alexander's voice sent quivers of awareness cascading through Merry. Though she knew Alexander hadn't intended to sound seductive, with moonlight spilling around them, bathing him in an ethereal glow, everything seemed sensual. The atmosphere was charged with a sizzle that hummed along her skin. The fact that Alexander was wearing one measly piece of clothing didn't help.

Of course, since La Torchere's owner had made it clear that he didn't like her, Merry knew any romance she might be feeling was all in her imagination. She swallowed and took a pace back. "Yeah. Just you and me."

He gave her a curious look. "Are you afraid of me?"

She laughed. "Of course I'm afraid of you. You're my boss. You could fire me."

"But you said today that you couldn't stay for more than the time you promised your dad. There's no reason to be concerned about a job that you'll be leaving in eighteen days."

"There is if I want to do it well." She paused and caught his gaze to convey her sincerity. "And I do."

He smiled, then shook his head. "I would have never guessed that."

She glanced up sharply. Sexual tension aside, this man hadn't liked her from their first meeting at the hotel desk. And she knew that was because he wanted Merry

Montrose back. If she didn't force him to see her as competent, it wouldn't matter who she hired. He would never accept that person, and he would spend the rest of his life looking for a manager who didn't exist. He might even follow her to Silestia where he could stir up a real hornet's nest of trouble.

"You know what your problem is? You jump to conclusions. You met me three days ago and instantly decided you didn't like me. You didn't even try to get to know me."

"We can fix that. We're here now. And alone. We can get to know each other very well."

That wasn't the response Princess Meredith was expecting. Worse, his voice sounded sexy and seductive again. She took another step back. "I don't think so."

He frowned. "You just said I wasn't being fair to you. So I'm giving you a chance to fix that. But you don't want it?"

"Most bosses don't get to know their employees at secluded pools."

"I don't see why not." He glanced around. "If nothing else, we have plenty of privacy."

Merry had no idea what he thought he was doing. Up to this point, he hadn't wanted anything to do with her, yet tonight he suddenly found her at a pool and suggested they talk. It didn't make any sense. . . .

Unless he'd changed his mind about the affair she'd tried to initiate. If he had, he was in for a big disappointment. If he only wanted to pursue their sexual attraction, she wasn't interested. All along she'd wanted romance from this guy, not a quick tryst.

And even if he wanted the romance, it was too late. If she took up with him now when everybody knew she was failing at her job, all the employees would gossip that she had only stayed employed by sleeping with the boss.

"I think I should get going."

"Why?"

She gaped at him. "What part of 'you're my boss' don't you understand?"

"My being your boss didn't bother you three days ago."

"Three days ago early departure numbers weren't up. Today they are. I don't want people to think I'd use a personal relationship to be excused for my poor performance."

Alexander only stared at her. Either Lissa was correct in saying that Merry had changed, or Merry was one heck of an actress. "What if I promise to be a perfect gentleman tonight, and promise never to mention this conversation to anyone? There isn't anybody to witness it, so unless you tell, there'll be no speculation about your work performance."

She drew a breath that expanded her chest, directing Alexander's attention to the fact that tonight's bathing suit was totally different from the little string number she'd been wearing the night he'd found her in his private pool. He didn't fully comprehend what was going on with Merry, but he did finally see that his betrothed was different.

And he also finally understood what Lissa had tried to explain that afternoon about why it was important for him to get to know the "new" Merry. From holding this one short, reasonable conversation with his betrothed, he'd learned she could actually argue without throwing a temper tantrum. She also didn't buckle under to pressure. God knew what other skills she'd acquired in the past seven years. If he was going to keep the upper hand with her, deal with her, negotiate with her after they were married, he'd have to understand all of her newfound abilities long before she knew she should be hiding them.

"You want to talk as boss and employee." She caught his gaze. "Nothing else."

Already they were negotiating. Alexander was smart enough to realize that he'd have to let her win this one. "Yes."

She sighed heavily. "Okay."

"Okay."

She drew a quick, nervous breath and glanced around. "So what do you want to talk about?"

"First, what do you say we find a place to sit?"

"There are tables," she began, pointing to the right where groups of tables were lit by track lighting along the fence.

But Alexander interrupted her. "Too bright. Besides, the chairs are uncomfortable. We buy them that way deliberately so people will gravitate to the pool."

"Chaise lounge . . ."

He shook his head. "It's hard to talk face-to-face when your chair has you pointed skyward. Let's get a blanket, sit on the ground and just relax."

"That sounds a little too personal."

"I already promised to be a gentleman," he said, striding to the white chest beyond the tables she'd suggested. He grabbed a resort blanket and walked to the soft grass some sunbathers preferred. Laying it out on the ground he said, "Go ahead. Pick something for us to talk about."

Still nervous, she glanced around again. "How about the resort?"

"The resort's a great choice," Alexander said, lowering himself onto the blanket. He knew she'd chosen that topic so they would talk business, but she'd unwittingly opened the door to the heart of who he was. He would be a fool to let it pass.

"There's a lot of money to be made in pampering people and I had . . . insider knowledge about some great spas and resorts in Europe. So I brought that knowledge here and, voilà, I made money."

"That's great," Merry said, easing over to the blanket, though slowly.

He patted the space across from him, encouraging her to sit as he continued to explain himself to the woman who would someday be his wife. "I don't think I'm great. I think I have common sense. I matched my existing knowledge with a need. It's a formula as old as the caveman."

She took a few more shaky steps. "It's an old formula, but I don't think it's that old."

Alexander almost laughed. He never realized nervousness made her picky. "Okay, how about as old as the steel industry?"

She stared at him. "Why are you selling yourself short?"

What? "Excuse me?"

"It's very clear to me that you worked hard to make this place a success." Angry with him, she absently sat on the blanket. "I'm guessing you worked equally hard on your other ventures because you like what you do. Success is a source of pleasure for you. But that doesn't mean you don't deserve everything you have, Alexander."

Alexander only stared at her, suddenly seeing he had been misinterpreting her. She wasn't nervous as much as she seemed to be getting frustrated with him for giving her such a flippant rundown of his life. Particularly, when she appeared to know the truth. The depth of her understanding of his personality stunned him into silence. She "got" him. She knew liking his work didn't diminish his efforts. She recognized he deserved what he had. He didn't have to convince her of anything, prove anything. . . . Hell, he didn't have to say anything! There was no need to explain his other financial holdings. He didn't have to tell her he had influence — or power. The woman who was to be his wife understood him.

He swallowed, overwhelmed with the feelings she must have been having all along. Without a clear-cut conversation plan, they were simply two scantily clad people alone at a beautiful pool. And, sitting cross-legged as she was, her knee was about two inches from his thigh.

He scooted away from her.

She glanced up at the sky. "You rarely see a cloud." Her voice was soft, breathless, as if she were totally in awe of what he had built on La Torchere. The appreciation in her voice turned the comment into a compliment and it flowed over him like the warm tropical breezes off the bay.

"Do you know that in some cities there's so much light you can't see stars? Yet here the stars go on forever. You were brilliant to choose an island far enough away from the mainland that it's unaffected by it."

He didn't want to be so pleased by her, but she was the first person who seemed to understand how discriminating he had been when he'd chosen this island, and he couldn't stop the current of pride that sizzled through him at her continued praise.

"You've got to be proud of yourself for preserving this little piece of heaven."

"I am."

"Legend has it you started with nothing."

"I did."

She laughed. "And for a guy who insisted we talk, you're very quiet!" She playfully punched his arm.

Alexander felt the slight touch resonate

through him. Not only did she understand more about him and La Torchere than he had expected, but also *his* Princess Meredith never would have joked. Yet this woman did. This Meredith — Merry as she had the staff call her — joked a lot. She laughed a lot. And he suddenly understood she was probably the reason the resort employees had been so cheerful lately.

"Come on, Alexander! Say something more than a two-word sentence!"

Knowing he had to really talk to her since he had initiated this conversation, he turned until he was facing her on the blanket. Bathed in moonlight, her skin was radiant, enriching the violet-blue of her eyes. Her plump lips were curled upward into a warm smile.

"What else do you want to know?" He intended for the question to be strong and firm, instead it came out soft, sensual, the question of a man to his lover.

Her smile grew. "Everything. Anything." She shrugged. "I don't care."

He swallowed and fought to remember why he wasn't supposed to want to kiss that sweet mouth. She was nothing like the spoiled princess he remembered. She was pretty, sweet, funny and *his*. So why couldn't he kiss her?

He caught her gaze and he could see she was thinking the same thing — or, if not the same thing, something very close. Her bedroom eyes called to him and made his fingers itch to skim along her smooth skin. He felt bewitched and remembered the rumors of magical powers held by the royal family of Silestia. He didn't believe in magic, but even if he did, he didn't think Merry was using anything but her natural charm to entice him.

She placed her fingertips on his cheek, almost as if she couldn't help herself, and Alexander stretched across the blanket and touched his lips to hers. Sensation after sensation buffeted him. Soft and airy, the kisses she placed on his lips weren't meant to seduce, but to show emotion. And Alexander realized something that astounded him. She *liked* him. She wasn't simply attracted to him. She liked him.

Confused, Alexander pulled back. She couldn't like him. She didn't know he was Prince Alec, and she had only talked to Alexander Rochelle three times. Not enough to have any kind of real feelings for him.

She once again touched her lips to his, even as she placed her palm on the back of his head and pulled him close to deepen their kiss. The tip of her tongue darted out and teased his lips. Alexander felt his control trickle away. When he opened his mouth over hers and she answered in kind, he began to fall over the precipice. Vulnerable, exposed, he let the thrill of intimacy wash over him until long-forgotten alarm shot through him.

The last time he'd let himself be vulnerable with Princess Meredith, she had humiliated him at her coming-out ball, and here he was doing it again. The only proof that she wasn't the same conniving princess who had embarrassed him was Lissa's opinion and a few well-placed comments about his resort. She could be faking her admiration, yet here he was falling under her spell. How could he be so foolish? Especially since this wasn't her first attempt at seduction. Had he forgotten the episode at his pool?

He pulled away so quickly he nearly lost his balance.

Lazy, drowsy, Merry said, "Alexander?"

Furious with himself, he cleared his throat. Before he could speak, he remembered the rumor of her family's magic again and for a second considered that she might have bewitched him, but, again, he dismissed it. He did not believe in magic. But he did know Princess Meredith was a conniver, and he'd nearly handed her the opportunity to get the best of him.

"I think it's time to leave," he said, pushing himself up and away from her, just barely controlling his anger with himself. When would he learn that this woman absolutely could not be trusted?

Chapter Four

Merry stood staring at the closed door of her villa. After several of the steamiest kisses she'd experienced in her life, Alexander had quickly walked her home and virtually dumped her at her door. But at least this time she knew he hadn't rejected "her." From the way he'd kissed her tonight — as if he couldn't help himself, as if he didn't want to stop — and the way he pushed back as if totally horrified that he'd let himself get lost in a few kisses, she knew he didn't dislike her. He disliked the power of their attraction.

Which made his behavior very easy to understand. If their chemistry was stronger than any he'd ever felt, he might question his ability to get out of the relationship as easily as he had his prior romances. Of course, the same intensity that confused Alexander reinforced Merry's intuition that she and Alexander really did have something special. But if he didn't want it, it seemed foolish for her to daydream about a romance with him. In fact, she was embarrassed by his constant rejection. A princess had her pride, after all.

Still, her yearning heart ached at the thought of giving up on Alexander completely, and her newly acquired maturity rejected the idea of succumbing to her princessly pride. She had no idea what it was about this man that drew her. She only knew that it saddened her to think tonight's kisses might be the only memory she would make with him — the only memory she would have to assuage her lonely heart while she fulfilled her duty to her country.

Alexander returned to his villa furious with himself. He actually wished he believed in magic, then he could say Princess Meredith had bewitched him and he wouldn't bear any responsibility for being out of control tonight.

He hit a few buttons on the phone sitting on the small table by his sofa. When Lissa answered he said, "I want you here in thirty seconds." Then he slammed the receiver into its cradle and strode to the bar.

After tossing ice into a glass with three clinks, he covered the shimmering cubes with Scotch. He wasn't the kind of prince who gave commands. Technically, with his family monarchy deposed, he wasn't really a ruler. So it surprised him that he suddenly needed to give orders.

He paused, the Scotch halfway to his lips. Actually, he didn't want to give orders. He wanted some answers and he'd only done what he'd needed to do to get them. He'd demanded that his best source for information come to his quarters.

A sharp knock sounded on his door, and he called, "Come in."

Lissa entered, wearing her La Torchere uniform, and he realized he'd ordered her away from night shift at the concierge desk.

"Your Majesty?"

Alexander scowled. "All right. I get it. That was a little heavy-handed. But this is making me crazy."

"What?" Lissa asked innocently.

Alexander groaned. "Don't pretend there's nothing going on. The woman acts like she spent the past seven years at Mother Teresa's convent."

"She didn't."

"So where was she?"

"That's for her to tell you."

He sighed. "She acts as if she isn't even herself."

"I keep telling you she's changed. She *isn't* herself."

"She's still a princess. Yet she hasn't once mentioned that to anybody."

Lissa smiled craftily. "You've never told anyone you're a prince, either. This is America. Not Silestia. Maybe she doesn't want to be a princess for a while, the same way you grew a little tired of being a prince."

Annoyed by the truth of that, Alexander scowled again.

Lissa took a few more paces into the room. "Come on, Alexander. Give her a chance."

"A chance to do what?"

She walked a little closer. "To prove that she won't be the worst wife in the world."

"Ha!"

"And maybe give yourself a chance to prove you're not going to be the worst husband in the world."

He turned and glared at Lissa. "My intentions were never in question."

One of Lissa's brows arched regally. "Really?"

"An arranged marriage makes your private life the property of the people. Our marriage will be a responsibility. I will fulfill mine."

"Without any benefit to yourself?"

"There is no place for benefit in a marriage where negotiations must take place.

That's why this charade needs to end. And end now."

Lissa studied him for a few seconds, then asked, "What has you so charged tonight?"

He scowled. "Nothing."

Obviously not believing that, Lissa studied him again. "Let's see, you're in swimming trunks, but your pool lights are off. . . . Where were you?"

As she waited for his answer, she obviously considered the possibilities and suddenly brightened. "You were with Merry!"

He tossed back the Scotch.

"And she's not at all what you were expecting so now you're feeling off balance!" Lissa crowed triumphantly.

"I'm not off balance."

Lissa ignored his denial. "Liking her could be a real problem in your marriage based on duty."

Alexander headed for the bar again.

Lissa laughed. "I'll bet you were ready to put your foot down with a spoiled princess and she's not spoiled anymore."

"I don't believe it. I think she's acting. Which means she's after something."

"Which means you have to spend more time with her."

Alexander smiled slyly. "Or confront her."

Lissa shrugged. "If you say so, Your Highness." She strolled closer to Alexander, who leaned against the bar. "But it seems to me that confronting her continues to give her the upper hand. If you really want to get the point across to Merry that you're not the same shy prince who was too tongue-tied to retaliate when she insulted you at her coming-out ball, this is your perfect chance."

Because she hit a nerve — *the* nerve that Prince Alec would carry with him until he died, *the* nerve that both hurt him and protected him from Princess Meredith by preventing him from even considering allowing himself to be vulnerable around her — Alexander knew he had to listen.

"The best way to show her the grown-up Prince Alec is by showing her the real Alexander Rochelle." Lissa shrugged. "You have nothing to lose and everything to gain."

Alexander would argue that any day of the week. He had plenty to lose. Not just his pride. There was a position of authority in jeopardy, too. Staying in Princess Meredith's company might provide her with plenty of opportunities to see he wasn't a backward prince, but being in her company also caused him to forget who *she* really was. She lulled him with kindness and tempted him with her body until he wanted to believe everything she said and did, if only to furnish himself with an excuse to give in to the sweet temptation of seducing her.

And he didn't know which was worse. Being out of control around her because of the shyness that had plagued him as a youth, or being out of control because of unrelenting physical need. Either way the power shifted to her.

"Unless you're afraid."

He sighed. "A child's dare, Lissa?"

"Are you afraid?"

He wished! The problem wasn't that he was afraid of Merry, but that he had no control around her. Technically, *he* was the problem, not Merry. "No."

"Well, since you're not afraid, my advice is to take tonight's events as a warning of sorts. Marrying Princess Merry won't be as cut-and-dried as you first thought. Particularly since you find her attractive. You could stay away from her, but that simply means you'll have to deal with being attracted to her when her father calls you to Silestia to fulfill the marriage contract."

She strolled away. "It seems smarter to me to handle it now. Instead of running from her, why not strike first? Be the seducer instead of the seduced."

Hearing his dilemma and a very good solution coming from Lissa, Alexander would swear the woman had been watching over their shoulders. How else would she know the real problem was that his sexual attraction to Merry erased his common sense?

He looked at the ceiling as if seeking heavenly counsel then said, "So you're suggesting I see her again?"

"But this time, don't spend the whole date fighting your attraction. Go with it. Use it. Show her how easily *you* could seduce *her*." She caught his gaze. "Marriage is a negotiation, right?"

He sighed.

"And you do have to sleep together to produce heirs."

He sighed again.

"You don't want to be the one without the power."

No. He did not.

Lissa strolled away. Her voice was darkly confident when she suggested, "Unless you're afraid she's not as attracted to you as you are to her. . . ."

"She's attracted to me."

"Prove it."

The next morning Alexander meandered into Merry's office. When she glanced up from her desk, he saw her unguarded look of desire before she could hide it and he knew he was on track. And that Lissa had been correct. The best defense against Merry's charms was the good offense of using his own charms on her.

"What do you want?"

He casually leaned one hip against her desk, half sitting and half standing to show he was comfortable, relaxed, in control. "To spend the day with you."

Dismissing him and his suggestion, she took a file folder and walked to the cabinet. "I'm busy."

"And I'm your boss."

"That's the argument for why we *shouldn't* spend time together."

"Not if you look at my request as an order from your superior."

She slid the file into its appropriate place then slammed the door closed. "Isn't that sexual harassment?"

"No," he said, deliberately making his voice contrite and sad. Lissa wanted to see sexual power? He'd show her power. "Actually, I want to make up for last night's disaster."

Merry slowly turned from the cabinet to face him.

"I'm very sorry that I ruined our time at the pool."

"You didn't ruin it. You just got angry for no reason and dumped me at my door like a sack of potatoes."

He had no idea when Princess Meredith had ever seen a sack of potatoes, but the analogy was a good one. "How about if I promise that I won't dump you at your door?"

Interest flared in her eyes and Alexander could all but taste victory. "You simply want to spend time with me?"

"That's it. No sexual harassment. No compromising positions."

"Where do you want to go? What do you want to do?"

That was the beauty of his plan. He had the perfect sport for wooing her without her even realizing she was being seduced. "I thought we'd play eighteen holes of golf."

She blinked. "Golf?"

"It's an activity where we'd be fully clothed, so I could prove to you that I'm trustworthy."

She frowned. "I don't think you're un-trustworthy."

"Perhaps not, but things did move a little quickly yesterday. If we'd gone any further, you might not have trusted me again."

She considered that, then shrugged. "Maybe."

"So . . . golf?"

She smiled sheepishly. "I'm not very good."

"Great, then I'll win."

She laughed. "Give me fifteen minutes to change."

"I'll meet you at the clubhouse."

Though September heralded the beginning of fall for most of the United States, the ninth month of the year was hot, clear and absolutely perfect in Florida. The grass was green. The sun high and bright.

With two sets of golf clubs tucked into the back of his private cart, Alexander praised himself for his cleverness. Not only were they once again alone at a resort where there was usually somebody sharing all of your activities, but also they were playing a sport that tested even the best tempers.

While waiting for her at the clubhouse, Alexander had reconsidered their moonlight kisses at the Oasis pool and realized the real bottom-line issue wasn't his sexual power. It was her behavior. With Merry acting like Gandhi's niece, he wasn't reacting the way he would with the real Princess Meredith. But if he could get her to lose her temper and throw a spoiled princess tantrum, then the cards would fall to the table the way they should be falling. He wouldn't be dazzled or dazed, and she wouldn't ever

97

get the upper hand . . . not even accidentally.

He teed up and took his first shot, a beautiful drive straight down the fairway.

"That was perfect!"

She might as well know he was a great golfer, too. "That's about my average drive."

"Well, you're about thirty times better than I am!"

Good.

She teed up and positioned herself behind the ball. Alexander's attention was caught by the long length of shapely legs exposed by her white shorts and the way her peach colored T-shirt not only hugged her breasts but also heightened the pretty auburn color of her hair. She was, without a doubt, the most attractive woman he'd ever seen, and that reminded Alexander of the fourth reason playing golf was a great idea.

The first was complete clothing. The second was the privacy. The third was testing Merry's temper. But the fourth . . . ah, the fourth . . . was the opportunity for intimacy. He might not need to demonstrate his sexual "power" but it wouldn't hurt to remind his betrothed of just how attractive she found him. On the golf course he could do tons of "reminding" without once looking obvious.

"Your stance is off," he said, ambling over to her. "Let me help you."

Standing behind her, he slid his palms down her arms until he could cover her hands with his. With his chest to her back, he leaned down and whispered in her ear. "Your hands are good. Wrists are perfect. Elbows are tight." He spoke the words with his cheek rubbing against her soft hair, but he refused to be affected by that or the light scent of her cologne.

"So that's all good, right?"

He heard the quiver in her voice and smiled to himself. He was a genius. "It's all good." He removed his hands from her arms and with a lover's touch glided them down her hips. "But you need a little more action here."

She stiffened under his palms. With her back to him, Alexander knew he could grin to his heart's delight because he guessed she wasn't offended, but affected by the way his fingers lightly kneaded the gentle flare of her hips.

"Remember, your hips have to pivot." As he explained, he rotated her bottom, mimicking the movement her lower body should make when she hit the ball. "Just like that."

The twist of her hips turned her entire torso and brought their faces together. Alexander smiled at her confused expression.

Having his hands all over her left her more than a bit shaken, bolstering his confidence.

He stepped away and directed her to go on with her shot.

She took a long breath, blew it out in a gust, and positioned herself in front of the ball again. Then, without warning, or even ten seconds to readjust her position, she pulled back and slammed the club head into the ball, which roared skyward as if it had exploded from a cannon.

"Nice shot!"

Her mouth fell open in happy surprise. "Oh, my gosh! Look! My ball landed beside yours."

He frowned, not sure he liked the fact that she could hit the ball as far as he did, then decided to chalk her exceptional shot up to luck. "Good for you!"

She jumped into the cart with renewed enthusiasm and bounced out again when they arrived at the appropriate spot in the fairway. Unfortunately, her chip to the green wasn't quite as accurate as her drive had been. Neither were her nine attempts at putting. With all the work she had to do to get the ball in the following five holes, her energy began to wane, her mood darkened and Alexander prepared himself for a tropical storm.

"Let's see. I have a twenty-seven," Alexander said after the first seven holes. "And you have . . ."

"Eighty-four."

"I thought you played golf?"

"I did!" she cried defensively, but she quickly collected herself. "Well, I used to. It's been awhile."

"I'm sure it'll come back to you," Alexander said, pretending to be sympathetic, but the truth was he was on the edge of his cart seat. Any minute now he expected to see her famous temper, and when it emerged, he intended to pounce.

She hopped out of the cart to tee up after Alexander hit another ball to the middle of the fairway. He couldn't have picked a better day to have such a good game. Not because he wanted to show off in front of her, though that was a bonus, but because it was another way to push her to the limit.

She teed up and took her swing. When her ball clobbered a nearby tree, Alexander fell to the ground, barely avoiding being hit by the ball as it rebounded.

"Should I try that again?"

Alexander lifted his head from the gravel beside the cart path. "Unless you want to play the hole behind us."

Merry faced him and began to laugh. Apparently, seeing him flat on his stomach, with his face in the dirt, really tickled her fancy. She laughed so hard that as Alexander picked himself up, she plopped down on the soft grass beside the tee.

"I'm so sorry about this, Alexander. Thank God you have a sense of humor because it really has been a long time since I played." She smiled prettily. "But I think golf is more fun when I play poorly. I haven't laughed this much in years."

From the sparkle in her eyes, Alexander could see the truth in that. Sitting in the grass, not afraid of staining her pristine white shorts, laughing like a child, she was absolutely gorgeous. And her laughter was contagious. Particularly since her game *was* funny. He also imagined *he* didn't look anything short of hilarious, falling to the ground to duck her shot. Chuckling himself, Alexander took the few steps to the tee and sat beside her.

"I'm awful."

"You're rusty," he said, unable to quell the need to comfort her.

She faced him and sincerely said, "Thank you very much for your patience."

"It's my pleasure." He gave the reply automatically, but he suddenly realized he meant it. She was funny, fun. And he hadn't laughed this much in years, either.

With their faces only inches apart, Alexander knew he could kiss her. Her violet eyes very clearly communicated that she expected him to kiss her. Not in the saucy, demanding way of the old Princess Meredith, but in a sweet, nearly innocent way that had him wanting to believe she really had changed.

Half seduced, half angry with himself for again believing she had changed, he pulled away. But not rudely as he had the day before. Being careful not to do something he would have to apologize for, upsetting the balance of power again, he rose from the tee like a man who didn't get the hint.

"Now that you've had a rest," he said, as he unobtrusively got himself away from her. "Your shot should be easier."

She smiled, then nodded as if she appreciated the second chance he had given her, and Alexander didn't know what to believe anymore.

Particularly since he suddenly felt like the villain. She was a nice woman with a sense of humor working to please her boss. While he kept trying to trick her.

But she never once slipped. She hardly even wavered.

Maybe it was time to believe what Lissa kept saying. . . . Princess Meredith had changed.

That afternoon Alexander took Merry sailing, then invited her to have dinner with him. After the meal he had catered in his villa, he directed Merry to the sofa. Soft music filtered from speakers hidden in the wall. Soft Gulf breezes flowed in through the open sliding glass door. Three glasses of wine had relaxed Alexander, but Merry was too confused to be comfortable.

Alexander had seemed surprised that she hadn't lost her temper on the golf course. The few times he'd laughed with her, Merry had the feeling he never allowed himself that simple pleasure, and it gave her great joy to be the one who broke the ice for him.

And that scared her.

She was really falling for him. Not just because he was the only man she knew who could be romantic on a golf course. Alexander Rochelle was simply a wonderful man. She knew from his dealings at the resort that he was smart and crafty, but she also knew he was fair. Generous with both his guests and his employees.

She knew he lived the life of a loner, and

though it was by his own choice, she now saw his was a difficult life. Yet he never complained. He knew how to make the best of whatever situation he was in. He was funny, romantic and so darned good-looking he made her heart hurt.

And he liked her, too. Though Merry knew he'd fought his feelings, their mutual attraction had won. He couldn't deny he liked her company and he liked her. Her reward for not storming away when he'd initially rejected her, for giving him a second chance, and for being patient, had been a wonderful day outside and a gorgeous formal dinner. Now she suspected she was about to experience what would be the most romantic lovemaking of her life.

So why was she nervous? Without a word, Alexander took the wineglass from her hand and set it on the table in front of his black leather sofa.

Edgy, she glanced around at the red-and-black decor of his villa. "This is really an interesting way you've decorated."

He smiled and inched closer. "So you've said at least four times."

"I'm just nervous."

He cupped her face in his hands and asked, "Why?" But he didn't give her a chance to answer. Instead he pressed his mouth to hers and kissed her as gently and thoroughly as a longtime lover. Heat exploded in her middle. Her arms were heavy and listless when she raised them to wrap them around his shoulders.

He released her mouth and trailed kisses from her cheek down her neck to her collarbone. "You're not afraid of me are you?"

More afraid than he'd ever know. But she couldn't tell him that. "No."

His tongue traced the neck of her T-shirt. "Good."

Shivery urgency consumed her. Like a fire, it heated her skin and melted her bones. She'd never wanted a man the way she wanted Alexander, but for the first time since she met him she began to feel this relationship was a mistake. Not because she wanted to deny her sexuality, but because she knew she'd never feel this way about Prince Alec.

Alexander was the kind of man who would set a standard and it was unfair to Prince Alec to compare him to something he could never reach. It would be better for her not to experience the highest standard and give Prince Alec the benefit of the doubt, and not force her husband to live in the shadow of another man.

She took a long breath. Swallowed. "Alexander." She surprised herself when her voice was nothing but a wisp of sound.

He stopped. "Yes?"

She licked her lips. "I can't do this."

Chapter Five

The next morning Alexander was furious. Not with Merry for rejecting him, but with himself, for always giving her the benefit of the doubt. No, if he really thought this through, Merry was behaving perfectly in character.

So he intended to work from his villa, but when he opened his briefcase to retrieve the documents he needed to prepare for negotiations for a new resort, he didn't have copies of the deeds for the three properties he was considering.

He strode to his office in the hotel complex, grabbed the appropriate file and retraced his steps, only interested in getting out unnoticed. But as he bounded through the lobby, Lissa spotted him. From the alert expression that came to her face he knew she recognized something was wrong.

She didn't stop him on his way out of the hotel, but after he'd had enough time to reach his villa and toss his file folder onto his dining room table, there was a knock at his door and he knew she had followed him.

Apparently, Princess Meredith's god-mother didn't mind risking her life.

"What?" he asked as he opened his door to her.

"That's exactly what I was going to ask you. What happened? For the first time in her life, the princess is quiet and you look about as happy as a bear with a thorn in its paw."

Alexander sighed. "Why don't you go talk to her?"

"I did. She thinks she's running from a crush on an American businessman. *You* know what's really happening here. That's why I came to you for the story."

"Ha!" he said, granting her entry only because he didn't want anyone overhearing this conversation. "As far as I'm concerned you could be in league with the enemy, so if you think I'm going to give you a complete description of her skipping out on me last night, you're nuts."

"She ran out on you?"

"I'm not saying it again."

Lissa frowned. "Did she run out like a thief escaping a burglary or like Cinderella leaving the ball?"

He stared at her. "You *are* nuts."

"Just humor me," she said, taking a seat on Alexander's black leather sofa. "Was she eager to get out because she didn't want to be with you anymore or eager to get out because she *did* want to be with you but knew she shouldn't?"

Realizing he wasn't getting rid of this persistent old bat unless he humored her, Alexander said, "When she left she was . . ." He paused and thought for a minute. "Quiet. Subdued in a way I've never seen her before."

"That's exactly how she was with me this morning." Lissa frowned, obviously thinking things through. "What were you doing when she ran out?"

He sighed. He didn't really want to tell her this, but now that she was here and they were talking, he could admit to himself that he did need to make sense of what had happened. Lissa was the only person he could talk to. "Actually, we were sitting right where you are." He paused, then added, "Kissing."

"She ran when you were kissing her?"

Alexander began to pace. "As if her feet were on fire."

Lissa considered that, then asked, "Did she say anything?"

"Just before she ran she said, 'I'm sorry.' "

"And you assumed that meant she was sorry she didn't like you?"

"And you don't?"

"Alexander, the woman is promised to someone else. She wasn't supposed to be kissing anybody, let alone kissing somebody she really likes."

He stopped pacing and gaped at Lissa. "She couldn't kiss *me* because she was being loyal to *me?*"

Lissa laughed. "Yes!"

"The only way I'd buy that would be if she hadn't slept with anyone else in the past seven years."

"I'd stake my life on it."

Alexander fell to the sofa. "Right."

Lissa smiled confidently. "I wasn't kidding. I would stake my life on the bet that your princess hasn't slept with anybody in the past seven years."

"If she's so damned loyal, then why did she try to seduce me by my pool the first night she was here?"

Unimpressed by his revelation, Lissa shrugged. "When Meredith first got here, she told me she would love to have a casual fling with you. But I think now that she's getting to know you she realizes she can't. Probably because she really likes you."

"Right. People always reject prospective lovers because they really *like* them."

"They do if they think they're falling in

love, and they're promised to somebody else."

He sighed. "Look, I can believe that she's 'evolved' enough to feel guilty about cheating on Prince Alec," he said talking about himself as if he were a third person because, in a sense, he was. "But she can't have real feelings for *me* as Alexander. She hasn't known me long enough."

"Some people fall in love more quickly than others."

He laughed and shook his head. "You forget, we're talking about *Princess Meredith.* The woman to whom I am betrothed."

"She's changed."

"But our situation hasn't." He stopped long enough to sort through his explanation. If he said this right he might convince Lissa to butt out. "When Merry and I marry, she won't be my wife in this relationship as much as she will be Silestia's representative to my country. Just as my parents continually bartered personal things to get what they needed for their countries, Merry and I won't talk, we'll negotiate. And she knows that as well as I do. So all this is pointless. She'll never have real feelings for me. Our destiny precludes it."

"I don't agree." At Alexander's confused look, Lissa added, "Think about it, Alec.

She already likes you enough that she feels spending too much time with you could lead to cheating on her betrothed. Who knows how her feelings would grow if you gave her the next week or so to get to know you."

"Without telling her who I am?"

"You can't. That ruins everything." She sighed. "Look, if I'm wrong, when she finds out who you are what you believed all along will happen. You and Merry will have your marriage of negotiation. But if I'm right, if spending time with the real you causes Merry to fall in love with you, then there's a good chance your arrangement could be something else all together."

His eyes narrowed. "You mean a real marriage?"

Lissa shrugged. "Maybe."

He laughed skeptically. "I doubt it."

"What are you afraid of, Alexander? That Merry will prove herself to you, or that Merry will fall in love with you? Either way, she won't be the bad guy anymore. You will, because you can't stop punishing her for something she did over a decade ago."

When Alexander didn't answer, Lissa added, "Look, I know Merry hurt you. I know she embarrassed you. You would be perfectly within your rights not to give her a chance to mend her reputation. But I know you a little better than that. You're fair. And that's really what's bothering you. You know the fair thing to do right now is to give Merry a chance."

Alexander sighed.

Lissa moved to the door, but then turned to face him again. "Or would you rather return to Silestia and be seen as an ogre who won't forgive their beautiful princess bride for a mistake she made when she was just a kid?"

Merry sat in the sun at a small corner table in the Greenhouse Café. The cup of coffee at her right and half-eaten bagel at her left grew cold while she reviewed guest applications.

As a crone she'd had a knack for glancing at the forms filled out by newcomers to the resort and immediately seeing common interests. But today she couldn't find two people who even looked suited enough to share dinner, let alone become a potential love match. Worse, with the number of early departures steadily rising, she expected Alexander would, any day now, begin clamoring for the return of nonexistent Merry Montrose.

Princess Meredith's time was running

out, but she couldn't bring in a new manager when the resort was losing guests and Alexander was pining for an old crone. Though she'd already interviewed four people and had somebody in mind, she had to get the early departure numbers down and prove to Alexander that Merry Montrose could be replaced before she actually hired someone.

Merry closed the folder and reached for a memo pad. Since matchmaking ideas didn't come to her automatically anymore, she decided to make a list of the things she'd done to create the twenty-one matches that had broken her curse. This should refresh her memory about how to get people together. Then the early departure numbers would fall. She could bring in her new manager and the new manager could please Alexander.

Alexander.

Just thinking his name made Merry's heart melt. She now knew beyond a shadow of a doubt that if she let herself relax with him, they could have a once-in-a-lifetime love. But she couldn't do it. She was betrothed. And he didn't really want a once-in-a-lifetime love. He *needed* one, but he didn't want one.

Walking her home from Rick and

Cynthia's wedding, when she was still Merry Montrose, he'd told her someone had hurt him. He'd said he was cynical, though happy with his life the way it was. However, from the sadness in his eyes, she knew that wasn't true. He might be content or resigned, but he wasn't happy.

But that would only be her concern if she planned to spend her life with him. Since her betrothal to someone else precluded marrying Alexander, his misconception about the state of his life wasn't any of her business. Her business was getting Alexander's resort filled with happy guests and then returning to Silestia to marry Prince Alec.

"Grab your things."

Merry glanced up. When she saw Alexander standing by her table her heart stuttered. Dressed in a dark suit, with his hair neatly combed and his blue eyes serious and intent, he took her breath away. But because even noticing his attractiveness was wrong, she merely smiled at him.

"I'm sorry. I didn't hear what you said."

"I said gather your things. I'm flying to Atlanta this afternoon to meet with the owner of some property I'm considering for a resort in Georgia."

"What does that have to do with me?"

"You're going, too."

"But I . . ."

"Your aunt would have been happy to give me her opinion on whether the existing building could be remodeled to suit our needs. But if you don't think you're qualified . . ."

She bristled. The knowledge and experience she'd gained as manager of his resort was her first real source of pride and self-esteem. She was very good and no one could take that away from her. More than that, though, she had to prove to him that her "Aunt Merry" wasn't the only person who could run this resort. "I'm perfectly qualified."

"Fine. I'll meet you at the private airstrip in twenty minutes."

Assuming they were taking a day trip, Merry didn't pack. She changed into a blue suit and heels, an outfit more suitable for a business meeting, and scurried to the airstrip. Alexander's new pilot, Mick, escorted her to the plane and seated her.

Glancing around, Merry noted that Alexander didn't own a fancy, homey jet as her father did. There was no bar, table or sleeping quarters. Instead, though the plush gray upholstered seats were roomy and comfortable, the plane was clearly more for efficiency than pleasure. So much like Alexander. His life was filled with possibilities and potential, but he was careful, cautious and only took what he really needed.

Still, that wasn't any of her business. She reached into her briefcase to get her list of matchmaking tricks so she'd have something to focus on to avoid talking to Alexander. If he had asked her along with him to lure her into a personal conversation, maybe dinner and then into bed, he would be sorely disappointed. She was engaged. And she was a hell of a lot stronger mentally than Alexander apparently thought she was if he believed he could trick her into a weekend getaway.

Alexander boarded the plane. "I see you made it."

Merry smiled politely and said, "Yes."

"Good."

He took the seat across the aisle and Merry shifted uncomfortably. Her suspicions about his reasons for bringing her along caused a frisson of alarm to dance along her skin, but she reminded herself that she could handle him. Unfortunately, the clean scent of his cologne drifted to her, bringing to mind how good it felt to be close to him, and she almost groaned. She liked him. Darn it! Her refusal to have anything to do with him wasn't about not being attracted. She was promised to someone else. He wasn't making things better for himself by pushing them together!

But through the short flight, Alexander didn't say a word, and Merry refused to initiate conversation because she was an engaged woman attracted to the man who seemed to be spiriting her away. Of course, if he really was spiriting her away, wouldn't he be talking? Flirting? If nothing else, glancing at her every once in a while?

Of course he would. So since he wasn't, that had to mean he wasn't spiriting her away. He *had* asked her along to work.

Great.

Really.

She wanted to prove to him that he didn't need Merry Montrose.

She was glad, she told herself repeatedly during the limo ride, that he no longer seemed interested in her. And during the quick walk from the curb to their downtown Atlanta hotel, she used the phrase as a mantra.

The clerk at the front desk directed Alexander to a private elevator and Alexander motioned for Merry to walk with him. They stepped into the plush car, he pressed the only button and they were whisked skyward to a penthouse suite.

The door opened on a room with thick off-white carpeting. The space was furnished with a long cherrywood table and chairs. Behind that, a beige print sofa and two mauve chairs were arranged around a round coffee table, making a comfortable sitting area in front of the window. A galley kitchen sat on the right. To the left was a door that probably led to sleeping quarters.

Seeing the setup — not a conference room, but a hotel suite — Merry's heart stopped. He *had* tricked her! He'd stayed silent through the entire flight and drive to the hotel so he wouldn't have to explain where they were going.

"What the heck do you think you're doing?"

"I told you. We're about to have a meeting."

"In a hotel room?"

"It's a suite and I booked it so I could get Mr. Rodriquez off his home turf."

Merry glanced around, not even slightly convinced. "I'm not supposed to think you brought me here for a weekend getaway?"

"A weekend getaway?"

"Stop pretending you don't know what I'm talking about!"

"I don't."

She gaped at him. Did he think she was stupid? "You have to be kidding!"

"I didn't get where I am by kidding."

The tone of his voice made her frown and she narrowed her eyes as she studied him. Standing ramrod straight, an odd undercurrent of something that seemed like anger simmered through his entire demeanor. He looked like a force to be reckoned with.

No. She didn't think he'd gotten where he was by kidding. Which meant she was wrong again. They were definitely here for a meeting.

Alexander removed a few file folders from his briefcase. "These are the property files if you care to review them before he gets here."

"Sure. Good idea," Merry said. As resort manager she was the person who knew what guests needed to be comfortable and what the employees needed to do their jobs. So yes, she should be familiar with the property files. She reached for the first folder. When she saw it contained a financial statement, she nearly closed it, but her eyes caught the bottom-line numbers. Mr. Rodriquez was losing money. Lots of money.

She almost said something. Then she remembered that every time she'd opened her mouth today she'd been wrong. Without comment, she closed that file and reached for another, curious now to see where Mr. Rodriquez was making costly mistakes with his resort.

A few minutes later Norman Rodriquez arrived. A short man in his late fifties or early sixties with thick dark hair and round brown eyes, he wore cargo shorts and a print shirt. To Merry, he looked more like a hotel-lobby worker than its owner.

Alexander didn't waste time on preliminaries. After he introduced Merry, he directed everyone to the uncomfortable-looking table rather than the thick sofa and chairs, and the negotiations began.

Norman, as he insisted everyone call him, talked about his resort and its many attractions. Alexander countered with the kinds of changes he would have to make to upgrade the grounds and the buildings. Norman offered to put Alexander in touch with a contractor who could do the work for next to nothing, but Alexander simply said he'd pick his own people.

The cooler Alexander was with Norman, the more agitated Norman became, until the hotel owner seemed to understand that he was here only to sell the property. He and Alexander would not be friends.

"I was hoping for an arrangement where I

could be something like a silent partner and receive a percentage of the profits from your new resort."

"I don't have partners."

"Just like that? No negotiating."

"No."

He said it with such quiet assurance that Merry was taken aback, until she realized that was a part of Alexander's personality. He worked well with people, but he didn't have partners. He enjoyed romance, but didn't fall in love. Once again, she was struck by how alone he was.

Apparently recognizing Alexander was an immovable object, Norman finally named his price. Because it was three times what Merry believed the hotel and surrounding properties to be worth, she almost spit out her soft drink.

Alexander simply said, "No."

"Look, I know the hotel's losing money, but the way you intend to run it, you're going to make a bundle. I want a piece of that."

"There's no reason for you to get a piece of that."

Merry gulped at the tone of Alexander's voice. She'd seen him be imposing and intimidating many times, but she'd rarely seen him angry. But by all indicators, if Norman didn't stop pushing, she was about to see Alexander pushed over that edge again.

"Come on," Rodriquez wheedled. "There's not another property like it in the area."

"There are three properties like it and I'm talking with the owners for all three. Yours is the one I want, but I could make do with either of the other two. Now, would you like to give me a realistic number, or should I move on?"

Rodriquez drew a breath and cursed softly. But he finally gave a number. It was still a bit higher than Merry thought the property was worth, so she was surprised when Alexander agreed.

Without saying anything further, Norman Rodriquez packed up and left. He might not have gotten what he wanted, but he most certainly received more than he deserved. While Alexander had snared the property he needed for a price he obviously considered fair. It was the most perfect example of win/win she'd ever seen.

Forgetting she wasn't talking to Alexander, Merry spun away from the door and faced him. "That was great! *You* were great."

Alexander began sliding files into his briefcase. "Now do you see why I wanted him off his home turf?"

Merry thought for a minute, then shook her head. "No."

"Because people don't cave in front of their employees and Rodriquez needed to cave. His original number was too high. His expectations were outrageous. But, more than that, he needs this sale. He needs this money."

Merry had been reaching for a file to help him repack, but stopped short. "You brought us here for *his* benefit?"

"You thought I did it for mine?"

"Yes!"

"Well, you were wrong." He turned and walked to the small table beside the sofa and picked up the phone. He hit one button and said, "Send up dinner, please."

"Dinner?"

"I assumed you ate a late breakfast at the Greenhouse Café."

"Yes."

"But neither one of us had lunch and it's —" he glanced at his watch "— almost seven."

Merry looked out the window and realized evening had descended. She pressed her hand to her stomach. "I forgot!"

"This is why I like doing what I do," he said, closing his briefcase with a snap. He walked with it to the door. "I lose myself."

Merry said nothing and he continued speaking as he returned to the table. "I didn't like who I was when I first came to America," he admitted quietly, seriously. "So I appreciated the opportunity to get lost in my projects, to forget who I was, where I came from. But an interesting thing happened. The more I got lost in my work, the more I realized I was becoming the person I wanted to be."

Merry understood that completely. Working at La Torchere had at first only been a way to make her matches, but her job had quickly turned into a way to forget — if only for a little while — that she was a crone. Running the resort had given Merry her first sense of pride in herself. *That* more than anything else was what had changed her, but before she could tell Alexander that, their meal arrived. The waitstaff laid utensils and covered dishes on the table, and stayed to continue serving.

Merry and Alexander ate duck and drank wine, but he didn't talk much and certainly didn't say anything personal in front of the hotel employees. Merry didn't really expect that he would, but after tempting her with tidbits of his life, he had her dying of curiosity.

As the staff cleared the table, Merry took

a seat on the sofa, getting out of everyone's way because she was jittery. By the time the elevator door closed on the hotel employees, she was absolutely positive Alexander wouldn't open up again. He would be as silent on the trip from Atlanta as he had been on the plane ride from La Torchere.

But Alexander didn't seem to be in a hurry to leave. He took the wine from the table and walked to the stereo system where he pushed a few buttons that sent soft music through the quiet night air. Then he meandered to the sofa, where Merry sat. "Would you like another glass of wine?"

Merry almost declined. Not only were they a tad too comfortable, but also it was late. They should be going home. Still, she'd been curious about Alexander for so long that she couldn't pass up the chance that he might talk again.

"Sure."

Alexander poured two glasses of wine and set them on the table, but he didn't join Merry on the sofa. Instead, he caught her hand and pulled her up and into his arms.

"Dance with me."

Merry didn't argue. Being pressed against Alexander's strong male form rendered her speechless. Her curves seemed to meld into him. Her blood hummed through her veins.

She could happily curl against him and enjoy the feeling of being held in his arms, but she knew dancing with him was wrong.

"This was supposed to be a business trip," Merry said, trying to slip away and failing because he tightened his grip. "That's the only reason I came."

"You're still afraid of me?"

"No."

"That's basically what you told me last night."

Her brow furrowed in confusion. "No. I never said I was afraid. I told you I couldn't fool around. And there's a reason for that."

"You hardly know me."

Oh, so that was what was going on! She pushed away and gazed into his soft blue eyes. That one comment explained the trip, the dinner and even his unexpected opening up to her. Alexander thought she'd run away the night before because she wasn't ready for what he wanted, and he'd assumed she wasn't ready because she really didn't know him.

"So you brought me to this business meeting to show me your good points?"

He laughed and expertly twirled them around, breaking their eye contact. "Essentially, yes. Were you impressed?"

Merry couldn't lie. "Yes."

"Good, because it's important that you know I don't back down and I don't often compromise."

Her brow wrinkled in confusion. With an attitude like that it was a wonder any woman ever took him for a lover — even temporarily. He made romance sound like a professional wrestling match.

She carefully said, "Alexander, I've always appreciated your abilities. I know you're smart. I know you're crafty. But that doesn't have anything to do with . . ."

"You know a few of my good traits," Alexander said, interrupting her. "But you really didn't know *me*. Now I'm beginning to feel like you do."

"You're saying," she said, sweeping her hand around to indicate the room, "how you do business, is all there is to know about you?"

"It's not *all*, but it's the best part."

"Maybe. But it's not the *important* part. The important part is how you feel inside, not what you do." She paused, and when he didn't reply, puzzle pieces fell together in her head. He said he'd learned not to trust at a young age. He said that was because someone had hurt him, and the puzzle piece that had been in front of her all along, but she hadn't seen until now was that his heartbreak must have been devastating for him to pour his life into his work.

"Tell me about the woman who hurt you."

Alexander almost groaned. Technically, Princess Meredith was asking him to tell her about herself. Normally he would have steered clear of this particular conversation, but with her pressed against him, causing him to experience physical responses that were making him crazy, Alexander decided it might be a good idea to give her his version of the story. If nothing else, he could remind himself why he shouldn't be getting too cozy with this woman who with a glance or a smile could make him forget she wasn't to be trusted.

"She was a woman I wanted to marry," Alexander began, careful not to say betrothed or anything too obvious, as he tiptoed into the story of how *she* had hurt him. "One night she said terrible things to me, including that she didn't love me."

"Let me get this straight," Merry said, giving him a confused look. "*You* were going to marry a woman who didn't love you?"

"I was young."

"But why would you marry someone who didn't love you?"

Again, not wanting to admit he was in an

130

arranged marriage for fear that would ring a bell of recognition for her, Alexander told only part of the truth. "She was very beautiful and I honestly believed there was enough physical attraction that love didn't matter. Though her temper tantrums were legend, I still believed we'd find a way to —" he almost said work together, but in the last second changed it to "— work things out."

Merry gasped. "Oh, Alexander!"

"I was naive." Realizing from her dismayed response that she understood the full import of how her bad behavior had affected other people, Alexander pressed on. "Until the night she told me I repulsed her."

Merry groaned. "What a horrid woman!"

"In fairness, we were both young and at the time I was an ugly duckling. I only grew into my looks in adulthood. And my family was in financial disaster. I wasn't a prize."

"What she said was still cruel!"

The expression on Princess Meredith's face was priceless. Alexander wondered how she'd react if he told her she was criticizing herself, but he knew this wasn't the time to reveal his identity. If he told her who he was while she felt sorry for him, his position with her would be forever weakened.

"Actually, this woman was much too young to realize how deeply she hurt me."

To his surprise, Merry nodded knowingly. "All right. That *is* an excuse. Youth is full of folly. Lord knows, I made my share of mistakes."

An odd sensation stole Alexander's breath. Her admission felt like an apology and seemed to bridge the gap between the princess he knew and the Merry who had re-entered his life. It explained why he liked this Merry when he hadn't liked the other. This one could admit she'd made mistakes.

Dazed by her, Alexander bent his head and touched his lips to hers. Not in response to all the things he was feeling physically, but as a celebration of sorts. As he tasted her lush, sweet mouth, he slid his hands to her back and pulled her tightly against him, enjoying every brush and press of their bodies. Their situation might preclude him from loving her, but, as Lissa had suggested, that didn't mean there couldn't be more to their relationship than negotiations. With Merry's admission, they had the beginnings of a very shaky trust to go along with their powerful chemistry. For now, that was enough.

Actually, it was much more than Alexander had ever dared hope they would have.

He combed his fingers through her hair, then let them glide down her shoulders. He explored her size, her shape, everything he could discover while they stood fully clothed, enveloped in soft romantic music. This truly was a new beginning for them. He had heard it in her soft admission about making mistakes. He now felt it in her kiss.

Pressed against Alexander, Merry was lost in a sea of sensation. Under the magnificent reverence of his touch, her skin blossomed to life. Like a thirsty flower begging for spring rain, she strained against him. Not at all sure she liked the intensity of their chemistry because it rendered her powerless. Still, Merry succumbed to it. Everything between them felt new, different. Even the kiss was different, as if Alexander had finally allowed himself to like her . . . not their chemistry, but her. . . .

The realization froze her. Not because she wanted to protect herself, but because she suddenly realized that if she and Alexander went too far, these new feelings he had developed would cause *him* to be hurt.

She pulled back. "Alexander . . . stop."

He looked as bewitched as she felt and Merry knew that she was right. If they made love, and she was sure that was where they were headed, Alexander would be hurt. She stepped away. Out of his reach.

"What's wrong?"

Merry walked to the table and stood with

her back to him while she caught her breath, then she faced him again. "Alexander, you think your flings are casual. . . . But have you ever considered what would happen if you fell in love?"

His features tightened. "I'm careful."

"I can see that, but just for the sake of argument. . . . What if you fell in love with me and asked me to marry you. What if I had to tell you no?" She caught his gaze. "You would be hurt."

His sharpened features relaxed and he smiled at her. "That's not going to happen."

"That's exactly what would happen." Merry drew a long fortifying breath before she said, "Alexander, I'm promised to another man." With the words out and her composure slipping, she pressed her lips together and gathered herself one more time before she said, "I would never do anything to hurt my betrothed and making love with another man would be a betrayal."

"Merry, I'm . . ."

"No, Alexander. Let me finish. I also don't want to be hurt myself. And making love with you would hurt me. I keep thinking about the pain I would feel going through my life remembering making love to you, while I was married to another man." She paused long enough to catch his gaze. "And whether you know it or not, losing me would hurt you, too. If we gave ourselves to each other, and then had to part, we'd both be hurt."

Alexander stood dumbfounded, realizing she meant everything she said. Her emotion was so intense he almost confessed who he was, but he didn't because he was bewildered by the sadness in her voice. He knew the minute he admitted he was Prince Alec, her walls would go up and she wouldn't be honest with him. That meant if he wanted to know the reason for her sadness, he had to get the story before he told her he was her betrothed. Or else he would go through his life aware that his wife had been hurt, but he would never know by whom. The thought sent an unexpected lust for revenge through him.

"Who hurt you?"

She smiled slightly, as if confused by his question. "No one."

He shook his head. "I don't believe that. There's something in your voice that tells me you know a great deal about how much love hurts, and that could only be because you were hurt."

Her small smile became a real smile. "Actually, everything I know about love I learned by helping Aunt Merry match-make."

Because he'd never before seen Princess Merry at La Torchere, Alexander knew her connection to Merry's matchmaking was secondhand at best. Phone calls. Postcards. Not actual experience.

"I'm sure you heard many things from Aunt Merry, but no one learns about pain secondhand. And I see pain in your eyes."

Merry tilted her head in question. "And that bothers you?"

He shook his head ruefully. "Don't think you're changing the subject. You're not going to hedge this one. There's something in your eyes that tells me you know a lot about pain, as if you had a heartbreak that took you *years* to recover from." *Like seven years. The seven years she had been away.*

She licked her lips, obviously stalling.

Alexander sighed. "I told you the biggest secret of my life. I told you about the woman who hurt me, why can't you tell me about the person who hurt you?"

"Because it wasn't a person!"

"Right."

"It wasn't. It was . . ." She shook her head. "Oh, Alexander this is such an odd story!"

"I've heard lots of odd stories."

"Yeah, well, this one is about the oddest."

"I can handle it."

She sighed. "All right. Here goes. I wasn't hurt by a person, but I did go through a very difficult time because I wasn't always the nice person you're getting to know."

Oh, yeah. He knew that.

"In fact, I was a bit of a spoiled brat. So . . ." She drew a long breath. "My godmother cursed me. She took away my youth, beauty and social status. I lost everything. And it hurt. It hurt so much that some days I didn't think I was going to survive."

Disappointed, Alexander fell to the sofa. Here he was, thirsting to kill the bastard who had hurt her, and she was making fun of him. When was he going to learn not to trust her? Probably never if he kept letting her tell him half-truths and then walk away. So this time he wouldn't.

"Great. I told you the biggest secret of my life and you're making fun of me."

Merry's eyes widened. "I'm not making fun! Listen to the whole story. I spent seven years cursed. The way I got my youth, beauty and life back was to make twenty-one love matches. I've been here at La Torchere for five years."

Alexander didn't believe she'd been at the resort. But that wasn't the issue. Even remembering the whispered rumors that the royal family of Silestia was guardian of some kind of magic, Alexander refused to believe Princess Meredith had been cursed. It was simply too ridiculous in this age of science to believe in magic.

Of course, the people of Silestia didn't think so. They loved the silly legend that their royal family possessed magic. And Princess Meredith was going home in less than two weeks. It wouldn't do for a member of the monarchy to admit to a seven-year holiday. But the citizens of Silestia would love to hear that their princess had been cursed. In fact, they would eat up the story of a curse as if it were strawberry shortcake.

Alexander suddenly understood what was happening. Merry was test driving the story she intended to take home to her subjects to explain her seven years away.

Not at all pleased that she was using him as a guinea pig, Alexander nonetheless let her continue, hoping she'd dig herself into a hole that he could use to trap her, to prove her explanation was nothing but fiction.

"As I watched those twenty-one couples fall in love, I learned what love was. I learned that sometimes it's as much about vulnerability and hurt as it is about joy. But I also saw that true love is worth it and that's why I won't steer you off track by letting you fall in love with me. *You,* Alexander, deserve true love as much as anybody does."

It got to him every time she claimed to be protecting him. He knew she was only spinning a yarn, but something about her voice still touched him. There was a passion, a vibrancy to it that couldn't be faked. No matter what her lie, the reason for it was that she didn't want to see him hurt, and he suddenly wondered if she hadn't created this fairy tale because her own pain was so raw that she couldn't yet discuss it.

He glanced up at her. "And what about you? Don't you deserve love?"

"Love is about joy, but it's also about duty and responsibility. Respect and tradition. I will love my prince, the man to whom I am promised. I may never love him romantically, but I will love him."

At first Alexander was so stunned he couldn't reply, then anger took over. "You're kidding right?"

She shook her head. "No. I intend to love Prince Alec."

Anger transformed into fury and Alexander knew he had to get the hell away from her. He rose from the sofa. "I think it's time we went back to La Torchere."

Merry didn't argue. She simply turned away. Alexander's anger became acute disappointment. Two days ago it wouldn't have fazed him to learn Merry was about to perpetuate the worst ruse of all on Prince Alec. But after her half apology, after feeling they might really be on the road to a genuine relationship, knowing she was about to use love to manipulate a man she believed to be a shy awkward prince who would fall at her feet, Alexander was so disappointed his heart hurt.

When was he going to learn?

Chapter Six

Angry that Merry had lied to him, but furious that she intended to try to control him with "love," Alexander wouldn't inflict his sour mood on anyone the next morning. He called the restaurant to have his breakfast brought to his villa and he felt safe, until he saw it was Lissa who delivered it.

"You're just like a big dog with a bone, aren't you?" he said.

"Too much is at stake here, Alexander, to leave this to chance. I have to referee," she said, pushing the room-service cart into the foyer and to his dining room. As she set the place mat and silverware onto the uncovered polished oak table, she said, "So how did it go?"

Not about to tell Lissa that Merry had admitted to the worst trickery of all — she planned to pretend to love her ugly duckling prince to manipulate him — Alexander focused on the other half of her deception. "She lied to me. She made up a story about a curse to cover her seven-year absence, something I'm sure your subjects will love to believe."

"And that makes you angry?"

"I'm not supposed to be angry that she lied?"

"How do you know she lied?"

"Okay. Whatever. She didn't lie. She was cursed. Happens all the time."

Lissa shook her head sadly. "You have no sense of the true wonder of the world."

"I believe in things I can see and feel and prove. The fairy tales your country spins about magic are stories for people hoping for miracles. I can tolerate that. But lies are criminal. They always have a purpose."

"You're a fine one to talk about lies. If Merry is stretching the truth, as you believe, she's lying to Alexander Rochelle, a man to whom she doesn't really owe any explanations about anything. While you're pretending to be a totally different person to a woman you know is your betrothed. Considering that you haven't told her your real identity, I'd say you're even."

Rolling his eyes, Alexander took a seat at the table. "*You're* the one who encouraged me to hide my identity."

"Yes, but you could have told her who you were immediately upon her arrival, long before I got in the picture. Yet, you didn't. So technically, *you* started this."

"Yes, well," he said, unraveling his linen napkin. "She ended it with her lie."

"Alexander," Lissa said desperately. "Think through why she would tell you that story. Because you're someone from whom she expects nothing, wants nothing, needs nothing, there are only two possible answers. Either her story is the truth or she was trying to protect you."

Hearing Lissa say what he had realized the night before, Alexander was flooded by the same warm feeling he'd had when he realized Princess Meredith pulled away from his kisses because she didn't want to see *him* get hurt. That flood was followed by another torrent of sensation as he remembered her half apology. And that torrent was followed by a whirlwind that stole his breath when he remembered how they had stood in each other's arms taking their first shaky steps toward trust.

The night before, he had never, not for one second, doubted that she had anything but good intentions — until she tossed the word love into the mix. Then he didn't believe her. Because he couldn't believe her. If he allowed himself to believe she would love him then the whole game changed. It was much smarter to distrust her motives. That kept everybody safe.

No longer hungry, he set his fork on the rim of his plate and pushed away from the table. "No matter what her purpose, this charade is over. I'm calling her down here this morning to tell her who I am."

Lissa grimaced. "Please don't."

Alexander gaped at her. "You can't have it both ways! You can't use the charade as a convenient excuse for Merry's lies, then tell me I can't tell her who I am. . . ."

"Alexander," Lissa said, her voice soft with pleading. "Even if you don't believe she was cursed, in telling you that story Princess Meredith actually revealed bits and pieces of her identity. That can only mean she genuinely trusts you. And if she trusts you, love can't be far behind."

"Love. Right." He sniffed. "I told you. There's no place for love in a marriage made at the convenience of two countries. It puts the party who loves — and her country — at a distinct disadvantage."

"I disagree. Love breeds harmony, unity, understanding. I think both countries would have a distinct *advantage* if the arranged couple became a love match."

Alexander shook his head in disgust. "You are such a dreamer."

Lissa studied him for a second, then said, "You know, Alexander, you and Princess Meredith might have a bigger problem than her supposed lie to you."

"I don't see how."

Lissa smiled. "Have you ever stopped to think what her reaction will be when you tell her who you are?"

"Yes. I think she's going to be stunned and somewhat embarrassed that she didn't recognize me."

Lissa's smile turned into a huge grin. "Really? That's what you think?"

"I take it you don't agree."

"No. Not even close. If she's really the princess she's been presenting to you, I think she'll be mortified at how she tried to seduce you, how she responded to your kisses and how she even tried to finesse you into believing she could run your resort when you knew all along she couldn't. I'm guessing she'll want to die of embarrassment. She may even tell her dad she doesn't want to marry you."

Alexander's chest tightened. He'd been so sure she would be stunned that he'd never taken her reaction any further. But Lissa was right. If Princess Meredith *had* changed into an honest, honorable woman, she would be appalled by his deception.

Luckily, he didn't think she had changed.

"If she hasn't changed," Lissa continued. "If she's still the spoiled, difficult princess you remember . . ." She paused long enough to smile. "You should sell tickets and set up bleachers for when you tell her, because that girl will do more than die of embarrassment. She'll slap your face. There'll be a tantrum the likes of which this island has never seen. And if you think that princess is going to marry you, you're really deluded. You'll be lucky if your country survives whatever revenge she plans for your trickery."

Lissa paced around Alexander, looking him over as if he were a slab of beef. "Unless she has good reason to be thrilled you're her prince."

Though Lissa had built a definite case for Alexander to fear Merry's reaction, her last comment only made him sigh. *This* was the person he should have been worried about manipulating him. "You mean, unless she falls in love with me."

Lissa smiled. "Precisely."

"I told you, I think that would make things worse."

"Yeah, well, I think you're just afraid."

"You've tried this ploy before, Lissa. And I've told you, I am not afraid."

"Really? Are you trying to tell me that you

146

haven't yet realized that falling in love with our princess means laying your heart on the line with the woman who has already broken it once?"

No. He hadn't. Because he didn't need to go there. There were already enough reasons not to fall in love with his future wife. He didn't need another. But now that Lissa had mentioned it, Alexander realized it was true. Staying out of the love trap didn't just protect his country. It protected him.

Lissa grabbed the handle of the room-service cart and wheeled it to the door. "Looks like you've got some thinking to do, Your Majesty."

Once a year Alexander treated the executive board of each of his business concerns with a week-long "board meeting" at La Torchere as a reward of sorts. Each member was permitted to bring his or her family and each was encouraged to play more than work. This week, the executive staff of his computer software company had traveled from Omaha to enjoy the resort. For the next seven mornings they would meet in Alexander's dining room/conference room and hold a fifteen-minute meeting to justify their presence, then he would let them loose on the facilities.

After he talked through his one-page out-line of notes, the four men and two women quickly said assorted thank-yous and good-byes as they eagerly gathered their files, re-ports and briefcases. Within seconds only Jerry O'Riley remained.

"I hope you don't mind," he said, glancing sheepishly at Alexander. Jerry was a thirtysomething computer nerd with brown framed glasses. Currently, he had a pocket protector pinned to his bright red T-shirt. "But I told my wife to meet me here. We're going boating."

"I don't mind," Alexander said, laugh-ing at Jerry's childlike enthusiasm. "But what are you going to do with your brief-case?"

"Oh," Jerry said, pushing his glasses up his nose with his index finger. "Your new man-ager, Merry, is meeting us at the dock. She's not only taking my briefcase back to our room, but she's delivering a picnic lunch."

At the mention of Merry's name, espe-cially in such a positive light, Alexander scowled. He had to spend the next few days avoiding her because Lissa was correct. He needed to think things through. But more than that, he knew a little time apart would help their situation. At the very least, it would look as if he respected Princess

Meredith's wishes and had stopped pursuing her. "That's nice of her."

"She's a *wonderful* person!" Jerry said. "My wife adores her."

Alexander scowled again. *Wonderful person. Right.* If she was a wonderful person, he was in trouble because he'd been duping her. Once he told her he was Prince Alec, the roles of their relationship would flip and she would no longer be the spoiled princess. He would be the deceiving prince.

Yeah. He was really hoping for that.

Unfortunately, if she was the wicked princess he remembered, the rest of his life would be a war. She'd hold his trickery over his head like a guillotine blade.

Of course, either way, when he admitted who he was, she could end their betrothal.

So his future was to become the wicked prince married to a suffering princess and to spend his life attached to a woman who would take every opportunity for revenge, or lose a marriage his country needed.

His life was in fine shape.

When Jerry's wife arrived — a nondescript brunette with brown eyes, wearing simple khaki shorts and a white tank top — Jerry fell all over her as if *she* were a princess. Alexander felt a wave of envy. The kid was a geek, a nerd, a guy who lived for computer software. It was more than amazing that he'd found someone, and every time Jerry saw his wife, the joy of that amazement shone in his eyes.

Alexander wasn't a geek. He could have any woman that he wanted. But he lived behind a wall built out of necessity. The reality of his life was that he could not be vulnerable — especially not with a woman who would be his wife.

He and Jerry were alike in that their respective problems could keep them from experiencing true love. But Jerry had overcome his shyness. He'd learned to budget his time so there was some left for a wife. He'd learned there was more to life than his talent and his work. Jerry had faced his fears and won.

After a few pleasantries, Alexander closed the door behind Jerry and his wife and cursed roundly. He couldn't be like Jerry. He couldn't force himself to face his fear. He couldn't be vulnerable and open with Princess Meredith because his country wouldn't get what it needed from this alliance. Particularly not if his betrothed seduced his secrets from him then turned back into the wicked princess.

Unlike Jerry, Alexander didn't have the

luxury of tossing his heart into the ring and praying that everything worked out. He needed this marriage. His *country* needed this alliance. He couldn't risk loving her. Too much was at stake. At the same time, if there wasn't something more than mistrust between them, she wouldn't give him the benefit of the doubt when he explained who he was, and as Lissa suggested, she might be embarrassed enough to call off their betrothal.

He sighed, ran his hand down his face and then strode to his bedroom to change into shorts and a T-shirt. The bottom line was he had to prepare Merry. He had to drop enough hints about who he was that she wouldn't be shocked when he revealed his identity. She would wonder why she hadn't seen it herself. More than that though, he had to find a way that she would be thrilled — not angry — to know he was her betrothed. And after two days of turning this situation over in his mind, the only thing he could think to do was to seduce her. After a few heart-stopping, earth-shattering, soul-melting lovemaking sessions, she would be happy to discover the man with whom she was so compatible sexually was also the man she was to marry.

It made perfect sense.

★ ★ ★

Merry was packing when the knock sounded on her villa door and she pretended she didn't hear it. Even when her caller became more persistent and the knocking became pounding, she ignored it. There was no need for her to answer her door. She had made her decisions.

Her letter of resignation was written. Not only was she a complete failure as a matchmaker without the crone's magic, but also seeing Jerry O'Riley and his wife when she delivered their picnic lunch had driven her to tears. They were so sweetly in love, and so appreciative of their happiness, it broke Merry's heart.

Merry knew she and Alexander could have this kind of love because, in their own ways, they were as desperate as Jerry and Wendy had been. Even though she and Alexander had only spent a few afternoons and evenings together, it was easy to see they understood each other. Each had a wall. Each had fears. Each lived with the reality of his or her own private prison. Hers was growing up as a princess, making her mistakes for an entire kingdom to see and critique. His was being too wealthy to trust that another woman wouldn't hurt him as his first love had. She knew that if they ever made love it would be explosive. Not because of their chemistry, though they had it in abundance, but because they truly cared for and understood each other.

But she couldn't have the love that called to her. She was promised to somebody else. And though she had thought accepting whatever Alexander could give her would make memories she could cherish for a lifetime, she now knew it would only sadden her for her loss.

It was time to leave.

"What are you doing!"

Merry looked up from her packing to see Alexander standing in her doorway. Dressed in shorts and a T-shirt, as if he'd decided to take the day off, he looked adorable. Strong, powerful, decisive, and yet casual and comfortable. So darned warm and real and wonderful that tears filled her eyes. She wanted what Jerry and Wendy had. She wanted to fall asleep cuddled next to him at night and awaken beside him in the morning.

And she couldn't. She drew a long breath, blinked away her tears and smiled. "The real question is what are you doing? My door was locked. How did you get in here?"

Alexander sighed. "I still have master keys."

Merry shook her head at her forgetfulness. She was the one who'd hired him when he'd masqueraded as a handyman. Still, there was no sense delaying the inevitable discussion. "I'm throwing in the towel. My Aunt Merry had talents that I don't have. So I'm giving you a break and letting you replace me."

"What?"

"I'm going home."

Though Merry had thought this news would please Alexander, for a few seconds he seemed speechless. He took several cautious steps into her bedroom and four times opened his mouth to speak, but clamped it shut again.

"I thought my leaving would make you happy. You didn't want to hire me. The resort's numbers are bad. Two days ago, I told you a story about a curse that you don't believe. You think I'm a nutcase." She paused and opened her hands in surrender. "You should be dancing on the table, happy that I'm leaving."

He combed his fingers through his hair. "All right," he said, then raked his fingers through his hair again, as if stalling for time to figure out what to say. "I didn't buy the curse story in the literal sense of the word. But it is possible that you had a difficult seven years that *seemed* like a curse. So technically, you didn't lie."

Merry laughed. "Oh, Alexander. I don't even know what to say to that."

"Then don't say anything and just hear me out. I gave you a rough time when you first signed on as manager. Typically, when I get a new employee they have sixty days before I start calling their screwups screw-ups. I didn't give you that sixty days."

Merry frowned. "You're giving me a probation period?"

"Yes."

Merry turned back to her packing. "I don't know what good you think that will do, but you don't need to offer it. I'm okay with having failed. I'm learning to accept my limits and still be happy."

"You don't look happy and I think that's because it's hard to accept your limits when you didn't really fail. I'm to blame for your doing poorly. I know I added to your learning curve by being demanding. So if you stay, I'll keep my nose out of the resort business and let you do anything you want to do."

She shook her head. "Thanks, but no thanks. Like I said, I'm learning to gracefully accept my limits. But even if I wasn't, I made a promise to my dad to come home as soon as I could."

Alexander frowned, then he said, "You're going home to get married, right?"

She nodded.

"And from what you told me last night, this is an arranged marriage?"

She nodded again.

"You're doing something you're not sure is entirely right for you out of a sense of duty and responsibility."

"Yes, Alexander," she said, avoiding looking at him by stuffing her new clothes into a suitcase.

"Surely, you deserve one little vacation before you commit to all that."

Merry looked up, finally understanding what he was doing. A little vacation could mean relaxation or it could mean exactly what she'd had in mind for him when she changed from a crone into a princess. "You want me to stay because you think you're going to talk me into bed."

He chuckled. "I hadn't exactly intended to talk you into bed, per se. . . ."

She took a few steps to where he stood and studied his eyes. "Now, *you're* lying."

He sighed. "I'm not lying."

"So you're telling me you never intend to sleep with me."

Damn but the woman made him crazy! He couldn't tell her he would never sleep

156

with her. For Pete's sake, they would eventually marry. But even if couched, his admission in a very vague "someday" he would sleep with her, she'd leave.

He sighed. "Look, how about if I promise we won't do anything you don't want to do in these next two weeks?"

She searched his eyes. "Do you mean that?"

"Yes, I mean that."

He said it with all the sincerity he could muster, but she still shook her head and stepped away. "Sorry."

He saw the determined set of her shoulders, considered that no one could have ever convinced him he'd be begging Princess Meredith to spend time with him, and finally said, "Okay, then, bring back your aunt."

She stopped packing. "What?"

"The only way I'm letting you out of the commitment to the resort is for you to bring back your aunt."

"But she's . . ."

"Tired? So you said. But I saw her the night she left. I know she was a bit out of sorts but she wasn't dying. Besides, this is a resort. If she wants rest, she can get it by the bushels here. Plus, I intend to hire an assistant for her."

He waited for Merry to reply, but all she

did was moisten her lips with her tongue. He watched the pretty pink tip as it gently glided along the shape of her mouth and felt the kind of stirring that it wasn't wise to feel in a bedroom with a woman to whom he had made a promise of purity.

"I can't bring back my aunt."

"Then you're bound by the three-week commitment you gave me at your first staff meeting. Keep that commitment or I sue."

Merry laughed. "Fine. My father will be happy to pay whatever you want to get me home."

"I don't want money. I want time. And if you don't think I can win that in a court of law, just watch how much of your time I'll eat up trying. . . ."

He read the expression on her face and knew that she recognized a lawsuit could consume months not weeks, so he pressed on. "The reason I need you or your aunt here is that I want to have a party. Something very elaborate. Something formal." He hadn't thought of it until just this second but he realized that a ball would be the perfect place to reveal his identity to her. "I want every guest who has a reservation for a week from Saturday to be informed that they are to be prepared to attend a ball."

"A ball?" She laughed. "Alexander, aren't balls for royalty?"

"We treat our guests like royalty." He paused, then smiled. "You do have the expertise to plan something like this, don't you?"

She nodded.

"Then grab a pen. I have some thoughts."

Merry looked at him. "You want to start planning now?"

"What better time than now? You're not leaving. I'm in the mood to do this. So let's call the head chef and have him join us. We'll start with the menu."

Merry opened her mouth to speak, but snapped it closed. Alexander smiled. It wasn't exactly a big victory, but at least he'd bought some time.

Three hours later, the chef's eyes were glazed from the enormity of his new assignment, and Merry was actually comfortable in Alexander's company again. His all-business attitude had impressed her, but so had his knowledge of planning something so formal. In the end, she wondered why she had been surprised about Alexander's level of understanding. A man as wealthy and well-connected as Alexander had probably been invited to many receptions, balls and galas.

Because it was late when they finished, it was growing dark and Merry was starving. Nonetheless, when Alexander asked her to join him for dinner, she refused.

"I'm sorry. I have to go to my office. Now that I'm not quitting there are a million details I need to see to."

"I'll walk you there."

Merry almost sighed, but knew the best way to deal with Alexander was to give in to his demands because he wouldn't stop demanding until she did. And there wasn't much that could happen on a well-lit walk to the hotel.

She locked her door behind her and turned up the cobblestone path, but Alexander caught her arm. "Let's walk by the beach."

"But I have to get back . . ."

"In one of my many arguments to get you to stay, I offered you some time to rest and relax before your marriage. Just take it."

She sighed and allowed herself to be led down the path to the beach. Luckily, she was still wearing the shorts, T-shirt and tennis shoes she'd been wearing when Alexander interrupted her that morning and she could walk on the soft white sand. With the moon rising and the sound of the surf echoing around them, Merry felt some of her tension ease.

"You asked me the other day about my past and I wasn't really forthcoming with answers."

She laughed and pushed a breeze-blown strand of hair from her face. "No kidding."

"I'd like to tell you some things about me."

Surprised, but cautious, Merry said, "Okay."

"My parents had an unusual relationship. At the time they married, they were both . . . wealthy . . . and they went into the marriage with their own interests to consider."

She laughed. "Sounds like my parents. They basically married to formalize a trade agreement."

He peered at her. "Yes. That was very much like my parents' marriage. Anyway, because of some bad investment choices, my father lost most of their money."

Merry grimaced. "Ouch."

"And my mother wasn't happy."

Merry squeezed her eyes shut as pain squeezed her heart. In their last meeting she had told him she was promised to someone else and didn't want to hurt him. Now, he was explaining his background so she would understand why he'd made the choices he'd made and realize he had no intention of ever falling in love. She need not worry about breaking his heart.

He stopped walking and faced her. Merry refused to look at him so he caught her chin and tipped her face toward his. "Are you understanding what I'm telling you?"

"Actually, Alexander, I am. You're explaining why you've chosen never to fall in love. After living with parents who had a miserable marriage, the run-in with your mean-spirited first love finished you off. I get it. You don't believe in love."

"Yes, but there's more to it than that. I want you to know about my family."

"I don't see why, since nothing you tell me is going to change my mind. I'm not going to get involved with you. I'm betrothed."

She turned, ready to storm away from him, but he caught her arm. "I'm not asking you to break your engagement, only that you really give me a chance over these next few days."

"Why?"

"All I want is for you to get to know me."

"I know you better than you think. For instance, I know this is locked," she said, tapping his heart. "But I know that if you do open up and let yourself love, the woman you choose is going to be very lucky because you're nicer, kinder, more generous than any man I have ever met. But I also know who you are doesn't concern me."

With that she pivoted and began to walk away again. This time Alexander didn't attempt to stop her and instead walked with her. "Don't you even want to try?"

Merry stopped walking and gaped at him. "To what end? So we can sleep together once? Maybe twice? I already know I could love you, Alexander. And if we make love I *will* love you. Then I will not only short-change my husband, I'll spend the rest of my life pining for you."

Angry that he could be so thickheaded, Merry ran the rest of the way to the hotel lobby. At the front desk, she asked for and received her messages. As she reviewed the ten or twelve pink slips, Lissa sidled up to Andi Jones, the young woman manning the desk.

"Andi, how about taking a break?"

Andi smiled. "Sure. You don't have to tell me twice."

She left the front desk and Lissa caught Merry's hand. "Merry," she said softly. "The Phipps-Stovers are divorcing."

Confused, because she hadn't really been listening, Merry glanced up. "What?"

"The Phipps-Stovers are divorcing. You

163

don't have twenty-one matches anymore. As of two o'clock this afternoon when the divorce papers were filed, you have twenty."

Lissa looked absolutely stricken, which confused Merry all the more. "But they made the commitment."

"Yes," Lissa agreed, "but the commitment had to last at least until your thirtieth birthday."

Finally understanding what Lissa was saying, Merry quickly looked down at her hand and actually saw the knuckles wrinkle. The curse was back. She was becoming a crone!

"Oh, my God." Her eyes filled with tears and she pressed her fingers to her mouth. She couldn't do this again. Not again! Seven years as a crone were bad enough. Even another day would be torture.

"Merry, you need a twenty-first match before your thirtieth birthday or this curse becomes permanent. That only leaves you two weeks. But you can do it."

Merry's eyes filled with tears. She'd been trying to make matches since she'd become a young princess and had been totally unsuccessful. Yes, as a crone she would get her magic back, but would it be enough in a hotel where no two people seemed to even get along, let alone look like a match made in heaven?

The glass double doors swooshed open and Alexander walked into the lobby. "Merry, I . . ." he began, and though Merry longed to throw herself into his arms and weep, to get some of the comfort and understanding she knew he could give if he would simply open up, she knew she couldn't. He didn't believe in her curse. He thought her a liar. The man she instinctively knew would be the most wonderful listener and most patient partner, didn't like or trust her.

She pushed past him and raced to the back door, then down the cobblestone path.

Alexander made a move to follow her, but Lissa put her hand on his forearm and shook her head.

Chapter Seven

When Merry awakened the next morning, she glanced down at her hands and confirmed her worst fear. Thin, sagging skin covered her knuckles. A pale brown age spot had popped out near her wrist. She scrambled from her bed and ran to the mirror. Sure enough, tiny lines had etched around her eyes. Today the changes to her appearance were small. But if her transformation from young woman to crone happened at the same rate as it had the last time, tomorrow they would be obvious to anyone who looked at her closely. In two more days, she would be hideous.

She had only a few days — maybe four, but probably three — before she was Merry Montrose again, and two weeks to try to end the curse.

The night before, she had been shocked and upset. This morning, she was energized by an absolute refusal to let a curse control her destiny. Seven hard years had finally taught her how to be a good princess and she wanted the chance to be the kind of royal her subjects could look up to. She wasn't going to panic or roll over and play dead. She'd made twenty good matches. She could make another one.

She grabbed her phone and called the concierge desk. Recognizing Lissa's voice, she said, "Bring the guest list to my villa."

Lissa said, "I'm on my way."

Within five minutes, Merry heard the knock on her door. She opened it and Lissa waved the guest list at her. "Here you go."

Not wasting a second, Merry grabbed the computer printout from her god-mother's hands. "You and your darned curse!"

Though Lissa looked repentant, she said, "You didn't leave me a lot of choice. You had alienated your father and new step-mother, hurt Prince Alec, and weren't very happy yourself. I'd tried talking to you, scolding you, withholding new gowns and vacations. But that only made you pout all the more. In the end, magic was the only thing I had left."

"Well, magic might have worked for you, but I think *that* was the problem with the Phipps-Stovers."

Lissa's brow wrinkled. "You do?"

"Yes! It worked so well that I think it over-shadowed reality, and two unsuited people got married."

Lissa sighed her understanding. "That's why you asked for the guest list. You're not going to try to reunite the Phipps-Stovers."

"Without magic, they didn't last. It wouldn't be fair to put them back together again."

"Starting over with two new people doesn't panic you?" Lissa asked, a hint of confusion in her voice.

Merry sighed, wondering what the heck had her godmother so baffled. Putting two new people together was the only logical way to approach this. "I don't have time to be panicked."

Lissa strolled to the sliding glass doors and stared out at the bay. "That's actually my point. If you don't make that match before your birthday, you don't get another chance. If you're a crone on your birthday, you stay a crone."

Since it was idiotic to waste precious time talking about how little of it she had, Merry went back to examining her guest list. "I more than remember that from my first go-around."

Lissa looked out at the bay again. "I thought seven years gave you plenty of time.

I never realized your fate would come down to the wire like this."

Growing tired of a conversation that did nothing but rapidly deplete her dwindling minutes, Merry walked to Lissa and turned her godmother around until she was facing the villa door. "Much as I'd like to spend a good hour ranting and raving and shaking you silly for this moronic predicament you put me in, I have work to do."

When Lissa was out of sight of Merry's villa, she stopped for a deep drink of air. Even when put to the ultimate test — the failure of one of her matches and the reinstitution of the curse — Merry hadn't thrown a temper tantrum. She hadn't pouted. She hadn't hurled a vase, candlestick or centerpiece across the room. She wouldn't even take the easy way out by trying to talk the Phipps-Stovers into staying together.

The curse had worked! Her goddaughter had changed completely.

The only problem was, Merry really did only have two weeks to make another match. Remembering that, Lissa's chest tightened. Two weeks wasn't a lot of time.

She hoped Merry knew what she was doing.

★ ★ ★

If there was one thing Merry had learned about being cursed, it was that when your luck shifted from good to bad it pulled out all the stops. Two of her staff members got into a fight. One of the hotel laundry dryers caught fire and ruined half the linens, and just when Merry thought she would shoot the next person who interrupted her, Alexander Rochelle called and invited her to dinner. She didn't have time to coddle La Torchere's owner, but she couldn't afford to lose the job that was her only venue for matchmaking. So when he explained that he needed to discuss changes for the upcoming ball, she agreed.

But not happily; she was becoming a crone! The only obvious alterations to her physical appearance might be a few streaks of gray hair, a few wrinkles around her eyes and sagging, ugly hands, but Merry worried that things could change in a split second. She could be standing right under Alexander's nose when she zapped back into Merry Montrose! No woman wanted to look hideous in front of the man she loved, and Merry planned to avoid having Alexander see her as a crone, no matter what it took. But if it did happen, at least he would believe her curse.

Preparing for the worst, she dressed in white silk pants and a long-sleeved white silk shirt. The outfit was somewhat sophisticated, until she added the gloves. But she didn't think Alexander would notice her gloves, considering that she was sure his attention would be focused on the big floppy hat she wore to shade her face and camouflage the wrinkles that might pop out in the course of the evening.

Walking to Alexander's villa with a big hat, sunglasses, gloves and long-sleeved shirt and pants covering ninety-nine percent of her body, Merry got a few stares. But nothing was more priceless than the expression on Alexander's face when he opened his door to her.

"Halloween early this year?"

"I'm trying a new moisturizer."

"And it can't be exposed to what? Air?"

She nodded. People would swallow a ridiculous lie faster than a little one. "Something like that."

He stared at her for a second, then said, "I'm not so stupid that I don't understand that you've covered yourself because you don't want me to accidentally touch you. Which really makes me feel wonderful. Am I so repulsive that you couldn't let an inch uncovered?"

Horrified, Merry gasped. "Oh, no! Alexander! It isn't you. It's me."

"Right."

"No! I mean it. You don't repulse me. I like you!"

"Then maybe tonight I want you to prove it. I want you to stay with me tonight. All night."

Merry knew her first thought should have been her betrothed, instead, all she could think about was Alexander and how blatantly male he was when he looked at her as if he couldn't live one more night without tasting her, touching her.

Her insides turned to Jell-O and she nearly collapsed against him, until she remembered that she was becoming a crone. She couldn't be naked in this man's arms. She couldn't let him see her, let alone touch her. If they decided to make love and her body suddenly changed, she would be mortified.

She swallowed. "I can't."

"Why not?" he asked, inching closer.

Merry felt a shiver that was half fear, half longing. If Alexander knew how much she wanted him, he'd take her in a second, and that would be the last time. He worried that she was repulsed by him, but if her body suddenly became a crone's, he was the one who would be repulsed. She took a step back. He countered with three toward her.

"I don't like games, Merry," he said, getting nearer still, so close he could almost touch her. "And we've been playing games since the first day you got here. I'm not letting you walk away tonight."

Panic officially set in and all Merry could think about was running. Then she remembered his reaction when she told him about her curse. He all but threw her out. She didn't want him to dislike her, to think she lied, or to believe the worst about her and kick her out. But if she mentioned her curse and he got angry and asked her to leave, at least she could preserve the memory of how much Alexander had wanted her tonight. And if she didn't try this ploy, he *would* seduce her. Then there was a high probability he would see her as a crone, and she would live with his look of repulsion forever.

She drew a long breath. "Alexander, you didn't believe me when I told you the story of my curse. So you're not going to like it when I tell you that the curse has returned."

"You know, Merry, that's a good one, but it's getting old."

He took another step toward her and laid his palm on her cheek. Warmth seeped from his hand into her skin and Merry nearly leaned into his touch. She'd been alone for seven long years. And she'd never wanted anybody the way she wanted Alexander. Never. Maybe if she kept the drapes closed and the lights off, he wouldn't see? Maybe she could have this one night?

And maybe she would fall asleep and he would wake up with Merry Montrose tomorrow morning.

She swallowed hard and backed completely away from him. She could tell him a million lies for why she wouldn't stay the night, but she knew they wouldn't deter him. He would find a way around each one. Plus, he was right. They'd been playing games since she arrived. It was time for the truth and nothing but the truth.

If he didn't believe her, that was his choice.

"I don't care if you don't want to hear this, Alexander, but I really was cursed." She slipped off her gloves. "Look. My hands are like the hands of an eighty-year-old. And see that little brown spot there on the back of my wrist? That's an age spot. Next week it will probably have fifty friends. The curse has renewed itself because one of my matches dissolved yesterday. Though the physical changes seem to be happening slowly, there's no denying that I am turning back into a crone."

Alexander nearly sighed with frustration. It was true her knuckles looked aged and there was a brown spot on the back of her wrist, but as a former handyman, he knew a harsh cleanser could make a person's hands wrinkled and rough-looking.

"Why are you lying to me?"

Clearly angry that he didn't believe her, Merry whipped off her hat and revealed the streaks of gray in her once-perfect auburn hair. But Alexander knew she could have gotten those streaks from a bottle. Or, better yet, since Merry seemed genuinely convinced she had been cursed, Lissa could have paid the salon to put something on her goddaughter's hair that wouldn't be seen at her appointment, but would cause gray streaks after repeated exposure to the sun. If Lissa had orchestrated this ruse, then Merry really could believe it and Alexander knew he wasn't going to argue her out of her belief or get her to listen to reason. He might be better to play along.

"Anyone who's made twenty successful matches shouldn't have trouble finding another couple to put together."

"But I will! Don't you see? I'm smarter now than I was in the beginning and I can't just match any two people willy-nilly! The Phipps-Stovers are divorcing because they are wrong for each other. I can't even imagine how painful this must be for them. And it's my fault! I have to be careful to match the right people."

Dumbfounded by what she said, Alexander couldn't speak. She would only make a match that she believed was a good match. She wouldn't make a shoddy one even to save herself. The woman who, seven years ago, only thought of herself now thought of others first. And strangers. She didn't personally know any of La Torchere's guests, yet those were the people she apparently planned to match. She cared about these strangers more than she cared about herself.

He frowned. That couldn't be correct. Plus, it seemed rather convenient that she was doing all this right under his nose. With Merry so convinced of this curse and so determined to break it, Alexander couldn't help wondering if Lissa had "resurrected" it so Merry would look for her match at La Torchere, where he would see her, and — at the very least — stop thinking his betrothed was a liar.

"How will you know you are matching the right people?" Alexander asked, sitting on his sofa, looking for a way he could show Merry this curse was nothing but one of Lissa's tricks.

"I have to get the feeling that in the end the two people will care about each other more than they care about themselves."

Alexander couldn't help it. He laughed. If Merry believed that, then Lissa had really done a number on her poor unsuspecting goddaughter. "Please. In the end, everybody puts his or her own interests first."

"You have a very sad view of life, Alexander."

And didn't *those* words sound familiar? Like they had come from the mouth of a certain godmother/concierge. "And maybe yours is too flighty. You accept love and curses and happily-ever-after as if they're normal. It's a wonder you've survived!"

Merry smiled sadly, as if disappointed in him. "Alexander, you told me this afternoon that you wanted to make changes to your ball. Can we get started with that?"

Equally disappointed in her, Alexander nodded. "Sure. Dinner's in the dining room. I dismissed Oliver. I thought we'd serve ourselves."

"I don't know if I have time . . ."

"You don't have time to what? Do the job I pay you to do? I would think that would take precedence over a 'curse' since you need your job at La Torchere to find the couple to break the damned thing."

Merry took a long breath. For a guy who didn't believe anything she said, he certainly remembered details and drew conclusions about it well enough to use everything to his own benefit. Still, what he remembered and what he believed didn't matter. She had accomplished her purpose. He was no longer asking her to sleep with him. She was a disappointment to him. And he was right. She did have a job to do. If she annoyed him enough that he fired her, she would have no pool of people from which to make her match.

"Okay."

Alexander began walking to the dining room. "Well, thanks for being so darned happy about it."

"I'm sorry."

"Can't you just give me a couple of hours of your company?"

Because it didn't look as if she had much choice and because he was talking about spending time together, not sleeping together, Merry nodded. She would eat, talk about the upcoming ball and leave as unloved as she'd been as Merry Montrose.

But Alexander surprised her. As sweetly as if she were still the young beautiful woman

178

he'd been pursuing for the past week, he seated her. They discussed unimportant things like the weather, then he suddenly switched topics and explained how his business concerns demanded that he live in the United States. Though confused by his choice of subjects, Merry let him talk. She needed her job. He wanted this night. In some ways she wanted this night, too. Though she had gray hair and sagging hands, and she could feel a bunion growing on her foot, she was still enough of a princess that she could pretend he loved her. She could pretend they were a couple, enjoying the intimacy of talking about their lives.

But when dinner was over, Alexander suggested they sit on the sofa and Merry knew she shouldn't stay.

"I'm sorry, Alexander, we should really talk about your changes for the ball so I can get going."

"You won't sit?"

"No. I'm getting nervous now. I need to get moving."

"Okay," he said, then activated a CD with a press of a button on a remote. "Since you need to move, we'll dance."

She almost said no. But the tiny part of her that knew how lonely she would be as a crone couldn't say no to an offer that might not ever come along again in her lifetime. Alexander opened his arms and she stepped into them.

When he pulled her close and pressed his cheek to her hair, she nearly wept. Because they had danced before, she was attuned to his style and they glided effortlessly along the ceramic-tile floor behind his sofa and in front of the sliding glass door. The blinds were open, displaying his pool. The blue water shimmered with light from a full moon. She couldn't imagine anything more perfect, more romantic, than this moment. She closed her eyes to savor every single nuance.

Music floated around her. She could feel the movement of his body as he shifted to the slow rhythm. His arms were solid and sure. But she no longer liked him simply because he was handsome or sexy, the things that had initially attracted her. Now that she'd had a chance to know him, Merry knew she liked him because he was smart, savvy, and maybe even because he was a tad pushy. He was funny and sweet. Dear to her. When she thought of laughing, she thought of Alexander on the golf course. When she thought of baring her soul, she thought of Alexander, because technically he was the first person she'd told of her curse. When she thought of kissing, she thought of how sweet his lips were, how good his kisses tasted, how he made her feel desired just by the way his mouth made love to hers.

Lately, when she thought of anything sweet, dear, frustrating, emotional, wonderful, she thought of Alexander and she couldn't imagine what her life would be like without him.

As she realized the last, Merry's eyes popped open, then she squeezed them shut in agony. She didn't just like Alexander Rochelle. *She loved him.*

Oh, dear God! She loved him.

And the curse wasn't the only thing keeping them apart. Even if she broke the curse by finding a couple to match, she couldn't spend her life with him because she belonged to someone else.

But as quickly as Merry thought that, she had another, more important thought. How could she marry someone else when she couldn't imagine spending her entire life with anyone but Alexander?

He twirled them around the floor and nuzzled her closer. Her heart thudded in her chest, her body tingled with need and tears filled her eyes. She couldn't imagine spending her life with anybody but Alexander, and that meant she couldn't marry Prince Alec.

She knew it with such a fierceness that she suddenly wondered if that wasn't actually the real point of the curse. Matching twenty-one couples, and accumulating at least twice that many failed couples, she herself had changed, but she had also learned many things. The most important was how difficult it was for two people who didn't click to make the sacrifices and do the work required to stay together. If she were honest, she had to admit she'd never clicked with Prince Alec. Though she was willing to make the sacrifices, she had forgotten something very important. He deserved someone to love him. And she would never love him. Not completely. Not romantically. Not the way she loved Alexander.

That, she was sure, was the real purpose of surviving her curse. To realize she needed to terminate her betrothal. Not for herself, but for Prince Alec.

She slid out of Alexander's arms. Turning away, she walked toward the curio cabinet where she'd left her pad and pencil. "Do you want to talk about the ball or not?"

He caught her wrist and spun her to face him. When he tilted his head in question, Merry knew he saw the telltale signs of her silent weeping. "Merry?"

Her crying might confuse him, but Merry

easily realized why her eyes had filled with the tears that spilled over and now rolled down her cheeks.

The real bottom line to her curse, her time at La Torchere and even meeting Alexander Rochelle, was to force her to see that she didn't love Prince Alec and shouldn't marry someone she didn't love. Not for herself, but in fairness to him. So she would do the right thing by Prince Alec. She would not let him commit to a woman who didn't love him, but this fairy tale didn't have a happy ending. The man for whom she was willing to give up her Prince didn't love her. She had fallen head over heels for him in only a little over a week. But he hadn't fallen for her. Not because he wasn't attracted. He was. She knew he was.

Alexander Rochelle couldn't love her because he couldn't love anybody. Just from the things he'd said tonight it was clear he didn't know how to love. That was why he was so attracted to romance. It was a cheap substitute for the lasting, permanent emotion he refused to acknowledge.

Chapter Eight

"I have to go."

Alexander blinked. "Go?"

"Leave." She shook off the hand Alexander had on her forearm and grabbed her purse from the curio cabinet beneath the mirror.

But he captured her elbow and stopped her again. "I know. You can't stay because you're promised to somebody else."

Merry smiled sadly. "I wish I could say that was the reason, but I've decided not to marry Prince Alec. I really like you, Alexander, and that makes me see that it wouldn't be fair for me to commit to him. He has a right to be happy. He has a right to know real love. And I'll never love him," she said, and her eyes filled with tears again. "Because I love you."

With that she turned and ran out of the door. Alexander couldn't have followed her if his life depended on it. His feet seemed to be frozen to the floor.

She loved him?

Loved him?

He ignored the warmth that expanded in his middle at her confession and decided Lissa had pushed her so far with this fake curse that she was confused. Really confused. So confused she not only thought she loved a man she hardly knew, but also she intended to call off their betrothal.

Knowing he couldn't let her do that, he strode to his bedroom where he still kept the keys from his stint as maintenance man and rummaged for the set for the utility room. Desperate times called for desperate measures. Since he didn't think Princess Meredith would give him a chance to talk to her again that night, he would simply shut off the phone lines. Then she wouldn't be telling anybody anything for at least the next twelve hours.

With her mind made up, Merry knew there was no sense delaying the inevitable. Running to her villa, she swiped at the tears that had collected in her eyes and willed them to go away. She wasn't a little girl anymore. She wasn't even a spoiled princess anymore. She was an adult. A *wise* adult. Her godmother had cursed her to teach her valuable lessons about love, but she'd learned the most important lesson by falling in love with Alexander Rochelle.

She couldn't curse Prince Alec to a marriage without love. *She* might be able to pick up the mantle of duty and responsibility. She might also be willing to make sacrifices. But she couldn't curse Prince Alec to a hopeless marriage where there was absolutely no chance she would ever love him.

Falling in love with Alexander had cursed her as much as Lissa's spell had. It almost made no difference that she was returning to her crone status. She would never love anyone the way she now loved Alexander. She would spend her life alone.

She entered her villa and barely paused to close the door before she hurried to her bedroom. She wouldn't buckle under the temptation to throw herself across the bed and weep. Instead she straightened her shoulders, picked up the receiver of her phone and dialed her father's private number.

Nothing happened. Confused, she disconnected and listened for a dial tone. There was none. She stared at the phone. Were the phone lines down?

She tried to call the front desk, but even the inter-resort phones weren't working.

She hung up and slumped with defeat until she remembered she had *the* cell phone in the nightstand by her bed. She opened the drawer and pulled out the phone, and, sure as heck, it was on.

Welcome back.

"Well, gee, thanks," she told the phone, knowing it was crazy to talk to an inanimate object, but the stupid thing talked to her first. "Am I going to be able to use you to call my dad?" she asked, but before the phone could reply, she continued, "Never mind. I forgot that under this stupid curse my dad doesn't recognize me. He doesn't even know my voice when I call."

He will tonight.

Merry's eyes narrowed. "Why?"

You're getting a bit of a break because it's so close to your birthday.

"A break?"

The whole curse hasn't kicked in yet.

Merry stared at the message on the phone. Then glanced at her hand, realizing that though she'd covered herself, preparing for a sudden physical transformation, no outward changes had occurred in twelve hours. "Why not?"

Your godmother put it on hold this morning when she realized how little time you had left.

"So she can change things about the curse?"

No. The best she could do was buy you some time.

"She got me an extension?"

If you call not zapping into a crone immediately an extension, yes. But she didn't change the end result because she can't. If you haven't made a twenty-first match by your thirtieth birthday, you'll be a crone forever.

Merry took a quick breath. "How much time have I got before the rest of the curse kicks in?"

I don't know. I have no clue what kind of an extension Lissa could give you or even what parts of the curse are delayed.

"So I could still zap into a crone at any second."

Yeah. Sorry.

"Great."

Call your dad while you know you still can.

Her inability to talk to her dad when she was a crone was another reason to immediately let Prince Alec out of their betrothal. This time tomorrow her dad might not recognize her and Prince Alec could spend his life waiting for a princess who would never return.

"Thanks for reminding me."

You're welcome.

"Right." With that she dialed her father's private number. When Charles answered she said, "Good morning, Charles. How are you today?"

He cleared his throat, still uncomfortable with the new Merry, but ever polite. "I'm fine, Mum."

"Could I please speak with my father?"

"Yes, Mum."

Merry waited only a few seconds before her father took the phone. "Merry? Did you call to tell me you're coming home?" he asked, his kingly voice booming through the receiver.

Merry grimaced, but wouldn't let herself back out of what she had to do. "Father," she said, using her princess-on-her-best-behavior voice. "Some things have happened and . . ." She paused as an eerie feeling overwhelmed her. A pain skittered down her spine and her shoulders bent. Lissa might have been able to slow her outward transformation, but the internal changes were happening right on schedule.

She drew a long breath and forced her shoulders to straighten as much as they could, physically fighting the curse because she intended to beat it. "I can't marry Prince Alec."

"What!"

Merry pulled the receiver from her ear, waited for her father to stop ranting, then said, "I'm sorry, Dad. But I can't marry him."

"You *must* marry him!"

"I can't."

"Why not?"

She couldn't tell her dad she had been cursed and was becoming a crone. In her last round with this curse, every time she tried to explain it to anyone her words came out as gibberish, and she wasn't sure she could talk about it now. Fortunately, the curse wasn't the only reason she couldn't marry Prince Alec.

"I've fallen in love with someone else." Suddenly the tears that had begun at Alexander's villa returned.

"What?"

"Dad, I've fallen in love with someone else. Someone really wonderful," she said, for the first time grateful that she had all these remarkable feelings for Alexander. She knew her dad would hear the emotion in her voice and believe her.

"And you're marrying him," her dad concluded dully.

Merry's heart broke. She almost whispered no, but knew that would only confuse the issue. Plus, experience with both the difficulty and unpredictability of the curse forced her to cover all her bases. If she didn't make her final match and remained a crone for the rest of her life, it would be

190

better for her dad to think she and her mystery man had run away to be together than for him to think she had disappeared for no good reason. Or, worse, for something he had done.

She swallowed the lump of sadness in her voice. "Yeah, I am. Actually, we're going to elope."

"Elope!"

"Yes. He's a wonderful man, Daddy. You're going to love him," she said. Though she was lying, she knew it was true. Her father would love Alexander's strength, his forthrightness, his cunning.

"Merry, do you realize what you're doing?"

She drew a quick breath. "Yes."

"I don't think you do. Prince Alec's country needs this union. His monarchy may be deposed, but the country still holds to certain traditions. You'll upset the balance of the economy of our region."

"Dad," Merry said, her voice beginning to tremble now as the ramifications of the rest of her life began to weigh her down. She fully intended to make her final match, but already having considered that she might fail, it dawned on her that if she didn't break this curse, she would *never* see her father again. She would never get the chance to explain to Prince Alec that she had put his country in a difficult position because she wanted *him* to find happiness. She would never get to marry anyone, have children, have a real friend.

"When I rebelled against your marriage to Mathilda you simply told me that you loved her and you had a right to happiness."

"Merry . . ."

"I have a right to happiness, too."

With that she disconnected the call because her tears began to fall in earnest now. For the first time since she'd been cursed, she was afraid.

Immediately after breakfast the next morning, Alexander reconnected the phone lines and returned to his villa to summon Merry. When he called her, she rudely refused his command that she join him and hung up on him.

Alexander stared at the receiver.

His first intention had been to reveal himself as her prince at the ball. Then, last night, seeing things had gone too far, he'd decided to tell her this morning in the privacy of his villa, where she could rant and rail all she wanted. Then, when she was done, he would lay everything out on the table and force her to stay with him until they worked this out.

But she refused to come to his villa.

And she had been rude.

Very rude.

He smiled. All this time Lissa thought spoiled, selfish Merry had changed. Ha! This was the moment he had been waiting for. Spoiled Merry lived.

He shoved the key for her office into his pocket, just in case she refused to answer his knock as she'd done at her villa the day before, and strode out into the sunny September day.

The moment of truth was at hand.

He bounded up the cobblestone walk, past Merry's villa and to the back entrance for the hotel lobby. As he entered, the roar of the fountain greeted him. So did several resort employees. He returned their hellos cheerily.

Finally! Finally! The truth was about to come out.

He marched through the lobby and down the corridor to Merry's office and knocked on the closed door.

"I'm very busy. Whatever it is that you need handled, send me a voice mail and I will handle it."

"No."

Alexander's one-word reply was greeted by silence. He waited a full minute and was just about to open the door with his key when he heard the click of the lock and the door opened a crack.

Wearing the big floppy hat that shaded her face, a long-sleeved blouse, long pants and . . . He stared at her feet in amazement . . . *boots*. Merry said, "How can I help you?"

"You and I need to talk."

"There's nothing for us to talk about."

"Actually, there's plenty for us to talk about. If you let me into your office, then the nice little crowd of employees who have gathered at the end of the corridor pretending to be working won't hear what we have to say."

She swallowed, and for ten seconds Alexander actually believed she wouldn't let him in. Then she sighed heavily, pulled open the door and walked away.

He stepped inside.

Facing the big window behind her desk, effectively presenting him with her back, Merry said, "I told you last night that I didn't want to see you anymore."

"Because of your betrothed."

"I told you I'm not marrying him."

"That's actually what we need to discuss."

"It's none of your business."

"It *is* my business." He paused, drew a fortifying breath and said, "I have a confession to make."

Merry spun away from the window. "Alexander, I don't want to hear your confession!"

"I know you think you don't, but . . ."

"But nothing! Alexander, are you so obtuse that you don't see that it hurts me to love you when you can't love me in return? I *love* you and you can't love anybody. Even if things weren't changing in my life, I wouldn't pound my head up against a brick wall by being with you when you can't love me. . . ."

"Merry, stop. I'm . . ."

She walked toward him. "I don't want to hear anything you have to say!" She grabbed his arm and turned him toward the door. "I thought you had a question about the resort. I wouldn't have let you in if I had realized you wanted to talk about personal things."

"But I'm . . ."

"Get out, Alexander!"

"Merry . . ."

"Stop!" she shouted, then with every bit as much passion, she suddenly asked, "Do you love me?"

Alexander took a pace back, feeling that he'd just been slammed with the ultimate trick question. If he said no, she would boot

195

him out without hearing him out. If he said yes, she would probably gladly hear him out and be ecstatic when she realized the man she loved was her fiancé.

But it would be a lie.

"It's a simple question, Alexander."

A week ago, Alexander would have agreed with that. This morning, he didn't. He glanced down at her face, but he couldn't see her eyes because the big hat shaded them. The shadow created was so dark he could barely make out the downward turn of her usually smiling mouth.

She wanted him to tell her he loved her because she loved him. A week ago, he would have thought it an empty phrase for a princess looking to have a good time, but today he knew it wasn't. Today he knew she believed all the hogwash Lissa had poured into her head about love, magic and happily-ever-after.

A little voice told him to stop obsessing and just do it. All he had to do was say "Yes, I love you," and *his* problem could be solved. It would be very easy to explain that he was Prince Alec after he told her he loved her. She would probably be overjoyed.

Was it such a big lie? He could straighten everything out just by giving her what she wanted.

But that wasn't really true. If he lied, he really wouldn't be giving her what she wanted. Because he didn't love her. He might be able to tell her that he loved her, but he'd never actually be able to love her. That one little manipulation of the truth would begin a lifetime of never really being honest with her.

The words stuck in his throat. He couldn't tell a lie that was essentially a promise he couldn't keep. He couldn't say he loved her and then marry her, condemning her to a life that was empty and lonely.

Suddenly he knew what he had to do, and he also felt everything he needed from this union slip from his fingers.

Just as Princess Meredith wouldn't marry Prince Alec when she didn't love him, he couldn't marry Merry, when he didn't love her. The very fact that she believed Prince Alec deserved better proved that she also deserved better. Certainly better than marrying the likes of him. And he hoped some day she found it.

"No. I don't love you."

She drew a shuddering breath. "Thank you for your honesty. Now could you please go? I have lots of work to do."

Chapter Nine

Merry's encounter with Alexander proved she couldn't bear the tension of not knowing when she would zap into a crone, and the next morning she ran to Lissa's villa and asked her godmother to explain the extension. But Lissa couldn't tell Merry what parts of the curse had been delayed and what parts of the curse were in full force. "I'm afraid I wasn't very specific. I asked only that you have access to the 'things you would need' to make your final match."

Leaving Lissa's villa, Merry logically assumed that everything she kept, like her physical appearance, must be necessary in one way or another to make her twenty-first match. And everything she lost, like muscle strength and strong joints, must be things not required for matchmaking.

Still, she wasn't taking any chances. For the next week, she stayed in her villa during normal business hours, afraid that her nose would suddenly elongate in the middle of a meeting, and worked after hours. Sitting in her office, listening to the muted roar of the fountain in the resort lobby, she could forget her troubles and put herself into the matchmaking mindset.

After reviewing the list of new arrivals each day, she would go out and mingle with the guests. Newcomers who had never seen her in the daylight wouldn't realize that her hair hadn't been gray the week before, her face had been without lines, or that the body that had once been trim and toned now sagged a little. All they saw was a friendly resort manager who paved the way for them to meet the cute guy at the bar or the gorgeous woman in the red bikini across the Oasis pool.

Unfortunately, despite Merry's enthusiastic introductions, after over a week of trying, she hadn't found two people suitable enough to share dinner together, let alone marry.

And she missed Alexander. By varying her schedule she had managed to avoid him, but that didn't dull the heaviness in her heart. The one man who needed someone to love and understand him more than any other would always be alone. By choice. He didn't believe in love and wouldn't allow himself to be vulnerable long enough for someone to prove tender mercies existed.

Sitting at her desk, reading the list of the day's arrivals, Merry reminded herself she couldn't think about Alexander. She had five days to match another couple or she would be a crone for the rest of her life. Her cell phone again worked magic. Incantations came to her as easily as breathing. She'd even caused an unexpected wave to wash up on the dock, forcing Amelia Giffin to jump back, away from the rush of water and fall into the arms of Kyle Martinez. But when Amelia and Kyle created a scene in the Greenhouse Café, Merry decided she didn't have time to fool around with matches that looked good in the short-term but weren't permanent. Most of her magic didn't produce long-term results, and she was now concerned that those short-term relationships did more harm than good. The Phipps-Stovers were in the throes of a bitter divorce. More than that, though, in falling so hard and so fast for Alexander Rochelle, Merry realized that sometimes the pain of losing a short-term relationship could be every bit as intense as losing a longtime love.

She refused to match some unsuspecting woman to a man who would put her through what Merry herself was going through right now. An ache in her heart, and not just for herself. No self-respecting woman could meet La Torchere's distinguished owner and not see the sadness in his eyes, hear the pain in his voice or recognize the emptiness in his soul. Yet, no smart woman could fail to see that Alexander wasn't trapped as much as he refused to come out of his self-made prison. Not even for her.

Alexander wanted her, but his fear of love was so strong that he couldn't even lie to get them both out of their uncomfortable last meeting. He'd told the truth and lost his chance to step out on faith. Which broke her heart.

So she would be very, very careful about whom she matched. No more Phipps-Stover mistakes. No more broken hearts.

The names of three sisters, Madeline, Mimi and Sophia Grasselle, ages twenty-eight, twenty-six and twenty-four, suddenly jumped out at Merry from the list and her pulse leaped in anticipation. With five days remaining to break this curse, she wasn't yet worried about making her final match. But she also knew there was no time to waste. Having three single sisters arrive all on the same day increased her chances of making a match exponentially!

She thanked her lucky stars Lissa had gotten her the extension that allowed her appearance to remain relatively untouched so she could still move among the guests as herself. She could go to the Oasis pool and scope out prospective grooms for these three lovely women without causing a stir.

The phone on Merry's desk buzzed and she absently punched the button to put her caller on speaker. "Yes?"

"I'm sorry, Merry, this is Renee at the front desk."

"What's up?"

"I have a gentleman here who doesn't have reservations."

"Do we have a room available to give him?"

"Yes, but he keeps asking for a Princess Meredith Bessart. He says he's her father." She paused, then added in a whisper, "And that he's a king."

Merry's eyes widened and she bounced out of her seat. *Her father was here!* Oh, Lord! Now what? She needed all her time to make a match, but she certainly couldn't ignore her dad! Not only that, but she hadn't seen him in seven long years and she'd missed him!

"I'll be right out!"

Merry ran up the corridor to the lobby, but with every step she took her leg muscles protested a bit more, reminding her that she was cursed, and interacting with her dad probably was not necessary to making her final match. So as with her original bout with the curse, she knew he might not recognize her. Still, she'd spoken to him by phone and he'd known her. She wasn't letting negativity cause her to miss the chance to talk to her dad.

When she reached the lobby, she saw her father and her stepmother, Mathilda, standing at the front desk. Though he was dressed in casual slacks and a polo shirt for comfortable travel, with his dark hair, dark eyes and regal comportment, Merry's dad was every inch a king. Similarly attired in casual slacks and a boat-neck sweater, Mathilda was also regal, beautiful, perfect, and Merry suddenly realized the full impact of their love. Her father had never looked this good, this happy, with her mother.

And *no one* ever looked so good to her! She knew her dad had come to the front desk himself because he didn't trust a servant to find his daughter. The seven-year separation had been as hard for him as it had been for her. He was so eager to see her that he put protocol on hold.

She cleared her throat and curtsied. "Your Majesty," she said, using the formal greeting she'd been taught as a child.

King Karl turned from the front desk.

"Finally, someone who understands decorum!" He took the two steps that separated them and put his hand on her shoulder, indicating she could rise. "Your name?"

Your name?

Merry's heart sank. She might look the same to everyone else, but something about her curse blocked her father from recognizing her and, as she'd already suspected, talking to her dad was not something necessary to making her twenty-first match.

She refused to accept this! She hadn't seen her father in seven years and she ached for him. He might not physically recognize her, but if she explained Lissa's curse and told her dad enough about their past together, she might be able to convince him she was Princess Meredith.

She cleared her throat, determined to give this a try. "Renee, why don't you take your break right now and I'll check in King Karl?"

Renee nodded, clearly eager to be relieved of the duty of checking in a king. "Thanks, Ms. Montrose."

"You're welcome," Merry said, taking Renee's position behind the desk.

Renee scurried away. King Karl said,

"You used the name my subjects use, King Karl. Do you know me?"

"I've actually been to Silestia." As Merry's fingers flew across the computer keyboard, she readied herself to try her plan. Though inability to talk about the curse was part of the curse, she had spoken to Alexander about it and her words had been normal, not gibberish. Which meant being able to talk about the curse must be necessary to making her final match. But that was good because that meant she could tell her dad, and unlike Alexander, King Karl knew of Silestia's magic. As soon as she explained the curse, she could tell him who she was and at least spend some time in his company.

"Really? Are you a friend of my daughter, Princess Meredith?"

Merry nodded. "Yes. You could say that." She drew in a fortifying breath. "Actually, I'm tree hormones dice flea."

Her father stared at her. "Excuse me?"

Merry's eyes widened, but she refused to accept failure. "I'm your groundhog baker sun ocean."

"Now see here, young lady!"

"I'm sorry, sir," Merry quickly apologized as tears filled her eyes. Damn it! It didn't seem fair that she could tell Alexander about the curse and not her dad. . . .

The thought made her pause in her typing. Unless being able to tell *Alexander* somehow helped in getting her last couple together?

Oh, Lord! It was so simple. *He* was the person she was to be matching.

In that second, with her beloved father staring at her as if she were a stranger and knowing her fate was to match the man *she* loved with someone else, Merry decided this curse was hateful. If she didn't match Alexander, she would lose her life and her father forever. But if she matched Alexander, there would be no point to getting her life back. She would have handed the only man she had ever loved to another woman.

Tears filled her eyes again, but she took a long breath of air to get through her father's reservations, typing as fast as she could.

Finally, he said, "Since you know my daughter, I'm assuming you also know where I can find her."

"Yes. She's here at the resort."

"Can you give me her room or villa number?"

She looked her dad in the eye. She couldn't tell him about her curse. Physically, he didn't recognize her. But maybe since he was expecting to find her here, she could talk to him on the telephone as long as she didn't mention the curse. She could explain any change in her voice as a cold, which would also get her out of meeting him.

"I'm sorry, I can't give out that information, but I will leave a message for her to call you. She probably won't get the message until morning," Merry said. "But I'll make sure she calls you."

The telephone was her only hope of talking to her dad again, unless she matched Alexander with someone. Then she'd have a lifetime with her beloved father, but lose the man she loved . . . to someone *he* really loved. Because the curse would not be broken unless Alexander truly loved the woman Merry found for him.

Because Merry worked until dawn, she slept until eleven. But she awakened surprisingly rejuvenated and in a much better frame of mind. She wasn't going to lose her dad or Alexander! Surely, her twenty-first groom didn't *have* to be Alexander. She could find two suitable people on an island full of singles!

Not wanting her father to think she was avoiding him, she phoned him even before she got out of bed. He didn't recognize her voice, but she told him she had a cold, then told him enough about her past to convince him she was his daughter. They talked for forty minutes and, again, Merry's confidence lifted. But when her father invited her to lunch, Merry remembered her limits. She reminded her dad of her cold, told him she'd see him when she felt better — which she would when her curse had been broken — and quickly disconnected the call.

She rolled out of bed, feeling stiffness in every joint and knew she couldn't let the lack of changes to her physical appearance fool her. Aside from gray hair, a few lines on her face, wrinkled hands and unsightly bunions on her feet, there may not be obvious changes she could see in a mirror, but inside she was changing. Lissa might have gotten her a reprieve of sorts, but it wasn't permanent. Her time was running out. She didn't even know if she would keep her good looks for the entire four days she had left. For all she knew she could zap back into Merry Montrose in the middle of a meeting, while wearing a bathing suit at the Oasis pool, or during a dance at the nightclub.

After brushing her teeth, she padded through her sitting room. Still deep in thought about the possible embarrassing ways and places she could change back into Merry Montrose, Merry jumped when she entered her kitchen and saw Alexander standing by her refrigerator.

"Where the hell have you been?"

Because she was dressed only in pink-and-blue plaid silk boxers and a pink camisole, she clutched her chest. "Alexander!"

"Don't Alexander me! I've left messages but you haven't returned my calls. I've summoned you to my quarters. You simply haven't shown up. Are you asking to be fired?"

Merry gasped. In all the confusion about the curse and what was changing and not changing, and then the arrival of her dad, she'd forgotten that annoying Alexander could cause her to lose her perfect matchmaking grounds. "I'm sorry. I've been busy."

"Doing what?"

She anchored her hands on her hips, deciding the best defense was a good offense. "Trying to manage *your* resort!"

She saw Alexander's gaze slide from her face to her neck, to her camisole and boxers. Now that his immediate crisis was over, it appeared he finally noticed she was scantily dressed. His gaze rolled down her legs to her bare feet, then made a slow return journey up, pausing on her face.

Again, the best defense seemed like a

good offense. "Don't say one word about my clothes! This is what you get when you surprise a woman first thing in the morning."

"I wasn't going to complain."

Merry's face puckered in confusion. He still found her attractive? She knew her wrinkles, gray hair, worn hands and bunions weren't horrendous, but a guy like Alexander surely liked his women perfect. In this state, she was far from perfect.

Still, the sunlight shining in through the sliding glass doors behind her could be camouflaging her crow's feet and highlighting the parts of her hair that hadn't yet grayed. Braless in a silky camisole, with her flaws hidden in the bright rays of the sun, she could have sparked his interest.

And dressed in his usual attire of a sport shirt and khaki trousers, with his hair ruffled from the breeze off the water and his blue eyes filled with fire, he definitely sparked an answering attraction deep inside her. Unfortunately, as quickly as she felt that, she got a surge of intuition. Alexander *was* the person she needed to match to break her curse.

The sudden surety she felt stopped her cold. With him standing in front of her, and her intuition running as high as she had ever felt it, there was no denying destiny. Alexander was the man she was to match.

She fought the urge to squeeze her eyes shut in misery and gruffly said, "I'm going to make coffee."

He whispered, "Okay."

Merry slid past him to get to her coffeemaker and she watched his eyes follow her, glowing with the sheen of sexual fire. She had to get him out of her kitchen. He might be attracted to her, but he wasn't in love and she was. She had deep feelings for him that made her want to do anything for him. If she weren't a cursed crone living in a twenty-nine-year-old's body, she might even gamble with making love if only for the experience and to have a memory. But she couldn't. To break her curse, she had to find *him* the love of his life.

"So where have you been for the past week?" Alexander's voice came from a few feet away and Merry turned to see him standing right behind her.

She wouldn't yell at him for crowding her. She couldn't even politely ask him to leave. She had to stay on his good side so she could be around him enough to pair him with the right woman. And *that,* she decided, was why the curse had let her keep her appearance. Merry Montrose had spoken with Al-

211

exander, but as young Merry, she and Alexander had a close, personal relationship. That was her ticket to getting him to take her advice when she introduced him to the women at the resort.

So instead of asking him to step back, she pretended his presence didn't cause gooseflesh to rise on her arms or her heart rate to accelerate, and casually said, "I told you, getting the early departure numbers down."

"But you haven't even been at your office. . . ."

"I've been mingling with the guests at night and sleeping into the afternoon."

"Ah."

"Though I haven't exactly made a match, guests have been having enough fun meeting each other that no one's leaving early anymore. Plus, I have my candidate now. I think I know who I'm supposed to match."

"This is about your curse, right?"

"Yes." She sighed, realizing that having him know so much about her and her curse meant she wasn't going to be able to fool him with a sneaky match. The first time she introduced him to a woman he would guess he was her intended groom.

"You know," Alexander said, strolling away from her to the counter, where he plucked a grape from a dish of fresh fruit.

"The easiest thing might be to simply bring back your aunt."

"I . . ." She almost said "can't," then realized that Aunt Merry would need this job. If Meredith Bessart didn't make her final match, she wouldn't be a princess anymore. She would be a crone forever. Without this job, life as Merry Montrose would be unbearable. "I did hear from her and you were right. She is getting bored in retirement."

Alexander brightened. "I told you!"

Merry smiled sadly. "Yes, you did."

But Alexander suddenly became serious. "I'm going to be very glad to get your aunt back, but that's not the reason I came here this morning. There's something else we need to discuss. Something I have to tell you."

The sincerity in his voice touched Merry's heart. She'd never heard Alexander sound so humble or contrite. She considered for a second that his feelings for her had grown, but dismissed that possibility. How he felt about her didn't matter. Once she found him a match, he would be off-limits. The final awful reality of her curse was that to become the princess she was supposed to be, she had to suffer the worst fate of all. She had to lose the person she held most dear.

"Alexander, I'm actually very busy today

and very much behind schedule. Could we save this for another day?"

"No. This is something I should have told you days ago — maybe even when I first met you — because it pertains to us personally."

Though it confused her that there might be something personal they could have discussed when he first met her, it didn't matter what he had to tell her. They were doomed. And she knew how to force Alexander to recognize that because she'd done it before.

"Alexander, do you love me?"

He sighed. "Merry, wasn't it hard enough the last time you asked this?"

"Do you love me?"

He closed his eyes wearily, then opened them and said, "No."

"Then we don't have anything to discuss. Nothing personal, anyway."

"You don't understand —" Alexander began urgently.

Merry interrupted him. "Really? You really don't think I understand? How stupid do you think I am? Your parents had a crappy marriage. Some little brat hurt you by publicly humiliating you. For the past several years, women have pursued you only for your money. You're jaded, Alexander. You don't believe in love and I do."

"Of course you do!" Alexander charged. "I might make fun of your curse story, but if you really matched twenty-one couples, you saw love twenty-one times. You know what love is. I haven't been that blessed."

Merry had never looked at her curse as a blessing before, particularly since it meant losing the man she loved, but in many ways she supposed she had been blessed by her seven years as a crone. It was a blessing that she could no longer be spoiled, selfish Princess Meredith. A blessing that she understood her father's second marriage. A blessing that she couldn't curse Prince Alec to a life without love. It was even a blessing that she was wise enough not to curse herself to a life with a man who didn't love her. In fact, it was even a blessing that she was willing to match him to another woman.

"I suppose I am." Saying that aloud, Merry felt her courage return and her spirits lift. He was the man she had to match and it was time to begin that process. "But Alexander, the curse is real." She stepped out of the sunlight, allowing him to see the lines on her face and the graying of her hair.

"Parlor tricks."

She shook her head. "No. A curse. A curse that's returning because one of my couples

215

divorced. But this curse is far easier to live with than the curse of being with someone who doesn't love you. And you don't love me. But more than that, you deserve love. . . ."

"I . . ."

She shook her head fiercely. "Look how close we came. You may not love me but you've talked with me openly and honestly. The next woman you meet could be the woman you will love."

Alexander felt his mouth fall open in horror and everything she had said that morning suddenly fell into place for him. "You're going to match me with someone!"

"I don't think I'm going to have to. I think you're ready to fall in love on your own. All I'm going to have to do is introduce you around."

He could feel his eyes widen with horror as he saw her walking him around the pool like her pet poodle. "No, Merry, I . . ."

She brushed him aside with a wave of her hand. "While the coffee is brewing, I'm going to get dressed."

With that, she walked out of the kitchen and to her bedroom, and Alexander felt the final straw break the back of their relationship. She'd refused to get involved with him as Alexander. She'd decided to terminate her betrothal to him as Prince Alec. Now she was matching him to another woman.

A man didn't need any more confirmation that a woman didn't like him, but Alexander never believed that being finally, unequivocally dumped by Princess Meredith would hurt so much.

He turned and left her villa. He was suddenly glad she'd blocked all his efforts to confess who he was. She didn't like him as anybody.

Chapter Ten

Alexander was gone when Merry returned to her kitchen, but it didn't matter. She knew what she had to do and now he knew, too. So when Merry not too subtly introduced Madeline Grasselle to Alexander, Alexander might have fumed, but he didn't embarrass himself or her by causing a scene.

Unfortunately, Madeline trotted off, looking for excitement. Alexander, it seemed, was boring. Disgusted, Alexander walked away. Merry went back to the guest list.

The next morning Lea Trusik and her cousin Stephanie Beyer checked in. Lea had all-American-girl good looks, with gorgeous blue eyes and long flaxen hair that hung to the middle of her back. Merry knew Alexander couldn't help but be attracted to either Lea or her cousin Stephanie, a tall, trim blonde with a perfect smile and infectious laugh.

But when Merry offered to introduce the two women to the owner of La Torchere, a gorgeous, available man, Lea politely refused. She took Merry aside and quietly admitted that they'd come to La Torchere for a rest because her cousin Stephanie, a doctor, had just had her heart broken and the two women were looking for sun, surf and maybe some tequila, but no men this time around.

Down to three days, Merry began to panic. But fate unexpectedly came to her rescue. The rumor had gotten out to the public that there was to be a ball at La Torchere and all guests were invited. Thursday afternoon, a plane-load of walk-in reservations arrived and the number of female guests was double what Merry had expected.

Every woman had thoughts of being Cinderella and finding a prince, and as quickly as the women arrived, the rumor began to spread that a real prince was attending the ball. Just in case, Merry scoured the guest list and when she didn't find a prince, she assumed the buzz was wishful thinking. Nonetheless, she couldn't seem to stop the persistent rumor, and suddenly no one wanted to meet the resort's owner. Everybody wanted to meet the prince. Everybody wanted a shot at being Cinderella. At the boutique, sales of clear acrylic slippers soared.

With her time passing, Merry suddenly realized she had failed. Every time she introduced Alexander to a woman, she walked away disinterested. And every time Alexander scowled and walked away, Merry felt success slipping away. Before she knew it, it was Saturday morning and she had only twelve hours left. Looking at her clock in disbelief, she knew that unless it was love at first sight for Alexander, she would not get her twenty-first match from him. In fact, twelve hours was probably too late to make a twenty-first match of any two people at the resort.

The thought seemed to trigger something inside her. Her joints stiffened even more, and when she passed a mirror in the hotel lobby she saw that her nose had grown to twice its size. Her neck had acquired two folds.

Holding back a gasp, she ran to her office. She'd prepared for this by keeping a long-sleeved pantsuit and big hat in her private bathroom. With no thought but to cover the changes in her appearance, she put on the new outfit. But when she looked at herself in the mirror, it was clear that even with the shading from the hat, she would not be mistaken for Princess Meredith ever again. The crone transformation was complete.

She was Merry Montrose.

She stared at herself in shock and disbelief. Never once had she believed, not even *once* in seven years, that she would fail. But she was twelve hours away from her birthday, eight hours away from the ball, and she wasn't going to make the match.

This, looking like a crone, talking like a crone, being fatherless, friendless, *alone,* was her life for the rest of her life. Worse, she now had to live in the same resort as Alexander, see his misery and realize *she* had failed him. She was the one who could have broken his curse by breaking her own, but she'd failed her assignment.

The ringing of her phone jarred her out of her thoughts. She grabbed the receiver. "Hello."

"I need you in my office."

Hearing Alexander's voice made Merry's entire body shake. She'd failed them both and she would spend her life helpless to do anything but watch their suffering and know she was the cause.

She swallowed hard.

"Merry, did you hear me?"

"I heard you, but I can't come right now. Actually," she said, thinking quickly and coming up with a very logical explanation, "I'm on my way to the airport to pick up my aunt. Merry Montrose is coming back."

"What?"

"I knew you'd be thrilled," she said, just barely holding back her tears. "And I have to go or I'll be late."

With that she dropped the receiver into its cradle and grabbed her purse. She had no intention of pretending to drive to the airport and no intention of saying goodbye to the staff. She couldn't say goodbye. Princess Merry no longer existed. If she tried to say goodbye, she would only confuse people.

Instead, she headed for the docks and took one of the boats. She'd failed in her mission and she'd hurt a lot of people. If nothing else, she wanted the one small indulgence of an afternoon of tears.

Because when she returned to La Torchere, she would be all-business Merry Montrose.

Alexander stormed to Merry's office, hoping to catch her before she left, but she wasn't there. Frustrated because the damned woman never listened to a word he said, he stormed out again and almost ran over Lissa.

"Where are you going?"

He drew a quick breath. "To find Merry. I just got word today that there's royalty at the resort and he's coming to the ball. That doesn't merely mean an entourage. It means special arrangements to give the man his due. There's no way Merry will be prepared if I don't find her right now. It's a mess."

Lissa wrung her hands. "It's a bigger mess than you think."

"Great," he said, running his palm along the back of his neck. "What else is wrong?"

"Merry . . ." Lissa began, but she stopped and gave him a curious look. "You're very stressed."

"I'm just tired."

"And it's only hours until your ball." She paused, obviously thinking. "You know, if I were you I think I'd take the afternoon off."

"I can't. I . . ."

Lissa smiled. "You need to be relaxed for your ball tonight. You should go sailing."

The thought of a sail suddenly pleased Alexander enormously. If Merry didn't want to take two minutes to hear that he'd just discovered her father was at the resort, then he would let her be surprised. Oh, sure, she'd be pleased to see her dad. But what wouldn't please her was that her dad had brought a complement of people . . . all of whom would be going to the ball. She would be fifty seats short tonight and, for once, he didn't give a damn.

"I think I will go sailing."

Alexander sailed to the three uninhabited islands off the coast of La Torchere. The first island was set up with private sporting facilities. Volleyball in the sand. Open spaces for Frisbee. Private sunbathing. It was a way for people involved in newly developing relationships to get real privacy. To ensure that privacy, time on the island had to be booked.

Not knowing if the island was booked, he passed it. He also passed "Island, too," as the resort employees affectionately called it. That island was equipped with hammocks, a shaded dining area and a lover's bungalow. In his foul mood, he didn't want to inadvertently see any lovers right now and he most certainly didn't want to "surprise" anyone in a compromising position. Instead he sailed to the third island, the island they hadn't developed in any way, shape or form and on which they'd posted hundreds of No Trespassing signs to discourage anyone from wandering over. There he knew he'd find complete peace and privacy.

★ ★ ★

After three hours of sitting in the sand, Merry still wasn't cried out. She couldn't shake her sadness or despair, not even by telling herself that life as Merry Montrose could have meaning and purpose. Nothing helped because she hadn't merely ruined her own life. She had ruined Alexander's life. Her father had lost his only daughter. And by failing to make her twenty-first match, she'd put Lissa in a position of knowing she'd doomed her own godchild.

Her failure had ruined many lives and she had to live with that knowledge forever.

Merry pulled herself up from her sand mound and slipped into her shoes. She had to go back. She had a ball to oversee. Tears filled her eyes and she didn't try to stop them. She dropped her big floppy hat onto her head and decided that she would cry during the twenty-minute ride back to La Torchere, then she'd stop. She would never cry again.

With one last longing glance at the beautiful ocean, she turned to leave and found herself face-to-face with Alexander. Dressed in cut-off denim shorts and no shirt, he'd apparently taken the afternoon off.

"I didn't hear a boat."

225

"I sailed," he said, but he was staring at her. "What in the hell happened to you?"

"You know who I am?"

"How could I not know who you are?"

"Because my own father doesn't recognize me."

He stared at her for a few seconds, then comprehension dawned. "This is your curse. . . ."

She nodded. "Yes, like I said I had to make twenty-one matches and I failed. But there's more. A few things you haven't quite grasped from our conversations. I've really been here for five years." She paused and drew in a long drink of air. "Because *I'm* Merry Montrose."

As if unable to believe what he was seeing, Alexander fell to the sand mound. "I need to sit."

"The curse is real."

He only stared at her and Merry decided to show him enough that he couldn't argue anymore. She took off her hat, revealing wiry gray hair, her wrinkled face and a nose the size of a small state.

"My God, Merry!"

"I didn't make my twenty-first love match. I failed, so I'll be Merry Montrose forever. You don't need to worry about looking for a new resort manager." She spread her hands helplessly. "I'm all yours."

Alexander let loose with a stream of profanity that would have melted ice and finished by saying, "This is ridiculous."

She shook her head. "No. It's a curse."

"You're going to look like this forever?"

"And live without love. I know I told you this before, but I was a very spoiled princess. My godmother thought she was doing the right thing by forcing me to change. I learned my lessons and nearly broke the curse, but that one couple . . ."

"The Phipps-Stovers who are divorcing?"

She nodded. "They separated and the curse returned. I tried everything in my power to get another couple together, but I just couldn't seem to do it." She paused and caught his gaze. "That means this is my fate."

"This *can't* be your fate," he snapped, so angry he couldn't believe he could feel such intense emotion. "Curses are antiquated and wrong!"

"They're a normal part of the system where I live."

"Then I curse where you live!"

She ran to him and caught his hands, pulling him up from the sand mound. "Oh, Alexander, don't! Almost a million people live in my father's country! Don't curse them!"

Frustration and anger balled in his stomach, but when he looked at Merry, at the pleading in her eyes, not for herself, but for her people, he knew she thought more of them than of herself. He also knew — had known all along — that she believed in this magic and seeing the proof standing before him, he had to admit he believed, too.

"There has to be a way around this."

"Yes, you could go to that ball tonight and let me try to match you to every woman there until you find a woman you love."

"You want me to fall in love in under four hours?"

"I've seen it happen."

He cursed. "No one can fall in love that fast, but I'm an even worse case than that. My God, Merry, we both know I don't believe in love!"

She squeezed his hands. "Oh, Alexander, don't worry about it. I can handle being Merry Montrose. Working at the resort actually gives my life meaning."

"So you're okay with this?"

She laughed slightly. "No! But I can force myself to be okay with it. What I can't handle is that I've hurt so many people and that I'll live my life not knowing my father or being able to visit my country. I'll never be more than friends with anyone. I will never be close to anyone. Not a man or a woman. I'll be with people, but alone."

He touched her face as if needing to feel the differences in her physical appearance for himself. "I won't let this happen."

She touched his face, as if for the last time, and smiled sadly. "You have no say in the matter."

"Of course I do. Merry, I'm rich beyond what you can imagine. I can do anything I want, change anything I want. There has to be a way around this."

"There is no way."

He studied her for a few seconds, processing everything she had told him, and finally, he said, "You said you won't have friends as a crone, but you can talk to me."

She shook her head. "God knows why and God knows for how long."

"Then marry *me*."

Merry looked up sharply. "Marry *you*?"

"Yes, it's the way around the curse. You might stay a crone, but you can talk to me. *I* can be close to you. *I* can be your friend. This can be the way you have a life."

Merry stared at him. "You don't know what you're saying."

"Yes, I do!"

"You're only saying this right now because you think you've found the way around the curse, but you haven't. Lots of parts of the curse haven't fully kicked in yet. This time tomorrow, I may not be able to talk to you about anything but work. Heck, I might not even remember you. . . . Or you may not remember our plan. You could wake up tomorrow morning married to a crone and not know why." She turned and walked away from him. "I won't let you do this."

He caught her arm and turned her around. "It seems to me you have no choice."

"I have plenty of choices. And my choice is not to drag another person down with me. I will not marry you. I will not curse you."

With that she turned and ran away. Alexander started after her but he tripped and fell. Every time he tried to rise, his foot caught on something and he was dragged down again, until Merry was far enough ahead of him that with her motor-powered boat it was clear that he'd never catch her.

He cursed roundly, then fell to the sand in misery. All along he'd considered his duties to his country in his marriage to Merry, but he never considered he also had a duty toward her until right now. But he couldn't discount the obvious. Her magic, whatever ability allowed her country to suspend the laws of nature, had prevented him from catching her, and it might be because of what Merry said. This time tomorrow he might not know her, he might not know their plan, he might have forgotten all about her curse.

If her country's magic could turn a beautiful woman into a crone, then it was possible it could cause him to forget everything he now knew and he would be in an awful situation in the morning.

He could handle it. Somehow he knew he would handle the embarrassment or fear or whatever might come over him when he saw he was engaged to a crone.

But what about her? Was it fair to risk her feelings? She'd been hurt so much that if he argued her into agreeing with his plan and then he left her in the morning, with no thought for her feelings, would it be the final straw?

Would that be the memory she'd have forever? The memory of the man she trusted walking away?

He couldn't do it. He had to let her live out her destiny alone.

Chapter Eleven

Alexander angrily dressed for the ball. All along his plan had been to wear his royal court attire, to reveal himself to Princess Meredith, but now that was pointless. Worse, revealing himself would do nothing but hurt the princess. He could not have her see that he was her betrothed, that the man she thought she loved was actually the man to whom she was promised, and realize everything she wanted had been at her fingertips. He might not have loved her, but she loved him and they would have been married, except for her curse. He couldn't deal the final, painful blow by letting her know who he was. It would be cruel.

He put on a tux and then sat on the Queen Anne chair by the French doors of his bedroom, steeped in misery and so angry he didn't know how to control himself. Eight o'clock became nine and nine began to inch toward ten. Yet, he couldn't seem to force himself to leave. When he realized how much time had passed with him sitting in a chair, he considered that her curse was again holding him back, preventing him from a possible love-at-first-sight encounter that might save her, but he soon admitted to himself that the truth was much simpler.

He didn't want to face her.

He didn't want to see her.

He didn't want to think about the fact that if he'd just once stopped to use some of his charm on any of the women to whom she'd tried to introduce him, he could have saved her from this fate.

That was what really bothered him. He could have saved her from this fate but he hadn't wanted to get involved with anyone. Not because he was betrothed to her and as loyal to her as she apparently was to him, but because he didn't want to risk his heart. There would never be a love-at-first-sight encounter for him. He refused to fall in love. Even after it was clear Merry's curse broke their betrothal, and he could indeed marry someone else, he wouldn't even try to fall in love. Not even to save her. He couldn't gamble with the pain.

It had been the story of his adult life. Princess Meredith hurt him, so he refused to get hurt again. And in refusing to get hurt, he had destroyed her. The bitter truth was, the curse was no longer to blame. In the final analysis of what went wrong, *he* was responsible.

It was just before ten when he rose from his chair, left his villa and walked to the lobby. He turned down the corridor that led to the back entrance of the ballroom where he could enter quietly, privately. He'd missed dinner. He'd missed the opportunity for a toast or words of any kind. He'd missed dancing with the women who were at the ball looking for a prince. He didn't feel much like a prince tonight.

Lissa awaited him when he reached the entrance to the ballroom. "Merry told me you asked her to marry you."

"Yes, I did."

The doors to the ballroom opened and a frazzled member of the waitstaff scrambled into the hall and to the door of the kitchen, apparently on a mission. In the few seconds of clear vision into the ballroom, Alexander saw Merry. Dressed in a pretty apricot-colored gown that would have brought out the beauty of her auburn hair and caressed every curve of her princess body, she looked almost silly wearing it as an aging crone. She also gave orders the way she had as Merry Montrose, quickly, efficiently, all business, and he wondered if she would even re-member who he was.

"She's almost fully a crone now."

Alexander peered down at Lissa. "I know. I also know it's you who cursed her."

"It was the only thing I could do. Believe it or not her life as Merry Montrose will be better than the life she would have had as a spoiled princess." She paused and caught his gaze. "I also saved you from a disastrous marriage."

"You can see the future now?"

"Sometimes. And I saw your marriage. You would not have liked your future."

"So you sacrificed her future for mine."

"Yes."

"Well, if that was supposed to make me feel better, forget it."

"You have to trust me."

The door swung open again and Alexander watched Princess Meredith scurry about, bent over, physically miserable. "Trust you? Right. All I have to do is look at Merry to know how trustworthy you are."

"Even as a crone, she liked you."

"What the hell is that supposed to mean?" he shouted, but he caught himself with a sigh and held up a hand to stop her reply. "No, never mind. I don't want to hear anything you have to say." With that he turned and walked toward the door to the ballroom.

When he had his hand on the knob, and

ready to turn, Lissa said, "It means that if you could talk her into marrying you, she wouldn't be unhappy."

His hand froze.

"She might not know who you are, but she would be happy."

He faced Lissa. "Would I know who *she* was?"

"I could fix it so that *you* always know who she is and that she's happy."

"So now you want me to give up my life for hers?"

"Yes."

He turned to go, unwilling to discuss this anymore and not sure he wanted to play Lissa's game. The rumor of the Silestia magic was obviously true, but that didn't mean it was benevolent as Silestia's subjects believed. Lissa's curse had failed and she'd destroyed her goddaughter. Alexander genuinely believed she should be punished for that. Instead, she was trying to rescue Merry by giving her at least a little happiness. As far as he was concerned, Lissa was pathetic.

Lissa caught his forearm. "Alexander, think it through. How much of a social life do you have anyway?"

"I don't really think that's any of your business."

"You asked her to marry you this afternoon . . ."

"Yes, I did. And now I'm glad she didn't accept. Because she told me that part of the curse is that she will forget her life. She won't have the torment of her memories. Which means she's not going to suffer. But *you* are." He pulled open the ballroom door. "I can't think of a better punishment for you."

As he stepped inside the ballroom, soft music hit him like a swell of the ocean. He wished with all his heart he didn't have to be here, that he could actually go to the Gulf and try to bring some peace to his soul, but he couldn't. He was the host. He'd missed several hours of his own ball already.

"Alexander!"

Alexander recognized the booming voice of King Karl, the man who should have been his father-in-law, and he turned to face him. Resplendent in his royal garb, he stood beside his wife Mathilda, a stunning woman in her red silk sheath.

He bowed. "King Karl. Queen Mathilda."

"Dinner last night was wonderful."

"It was my pleasure. I'm only sorry I didn't hear of your stay sooner."

King Karl brushed off Alexander's concern. "That's fine. Your staff has treated us perfectly. I especially adore your manager, Merry Montrose. Such an interesting woman. I loved her the minute I laid eyes on her. Something about her caught me."

Alexander didn't doubt that. "I'm glad everything meets with your approval."

"Yes, it does. I was just wondering though, what happened to the lovely young woman who worked with us initially? Her name was also Merry."

"She's gone," Alexander said, and glanced over to see Merry Montrose standing on the edges of the crowd, surveying the scene. To any onlooker, she appeared only to be doing her duty. To Prince Alec, she simply looked alone.

"That's a shame. I had a gift for her." He paused, then chuckled. "She reminded me of my daughter." His voice caught on the word *daughter*. "Princess Meredith is gone too. All her life she's been hard to understand. Seven years ago, she decided to go to school in America as a commoner. She finally called us from this resort three weeks ago. I spoke with her by phone a few times but it seems she's gone again."

Alexander didn't know how to respond. Words of comfort sprang to mind, but as Alexander Rochelle he wasn't supposed to know Princess Meredith and he wasn't yet ready to deal with King Karl as Prince Alec. He stayed silent.

"The next time she calls, I won't give her three weeks to come home. I'll find her."

"What if she doesn't want to be found?"

"She loves me," King Karl said fiercely. "I love her. And she now accepts my marriage. I don't know what's wrong, why she can't or won't come home, but I will do *anything*," he passionately promised, "change *anything*, to get her back."

Pain squeezed Alexander's heart. King Karl would never see his daughter again. Worse, he would spend his life with the uneasy sense that she was in trouble. Because she *was* in trouble.

The band switched tunes and a slow, romantic melody began. The King said, "Ah, one of my favorite songs. Will you excuse us, Alexander?"

Alexander bowed. "Certainly, Your Majesty."

King Karl walked away and Alexander searched the crowd for Merry until he found her. Again, she was alone. He took a long breath and strode over to her.

"Merry," he said, keeping his voice light and friendly. "Would you care to dance?"

"It's not appropriate to dance during working hours."

"You're not doing anything," Alexander said. "And besides, I'm the boss. You can't get in trouble with me since I'm the one asking you to dance."

He caught her withered hand and led her to the dance floor, realizing that when he'd danced with her at Rick and Cynthia's wedding, her withered hand had repulsed him. Tonight, it broke his heart. When they arrived at a clear spot, he paused and brought her hand to his lips and kissed it. Tears sprang to Merry's eyes.

Alexander felt his own eyes mist. But he broke the moment by pulling her into his arms and twirling them around the floor.

"Are you pleased with the arrangements?"

He automatically responded, "Yes." But he was feeling the oddest things. With her in his arms, he wasn't in the presence of a crone. He was in the presence of a princess. *His* princess. As he thought that, her face seemed to morph from crone to princess. The wrinkles disappeared. Her gray hair became auburn. Her violet eyes smiled at him.

He thought he might be seeing her as a princess because he knew her real identity, but suddenly he wondered if this was what Lissa meant when she said she could "arrange things" so that he would always know who she was. The rest of the world might see Merry as a crone, but he would see his betrothed.

He stopped dancing. "We have to go outside."

"No. If we're not going to dance, I have work to do."

He caught her wrist, but she held her ground, even stomping her foot. "No!"

People around them peered over to see what the commotion was about. He imagined they saw the resort's owner arguing with his old crone manager, and knew that if he married her this would be his lot in life. Everyone would wonder why they were together. Everyone would stop and stare. He would be a laughingstock. And Merry wouldn't even know who he was.

He took a deep breath. Maybe it was best to let well enough alone. He swallowed, then drew a quick breath. "I'm sorry. You're right, Merry."

She nodded her agreement, but when she looked up at him, he saw such sadness in her violet eyes that his chest tightened. She still knew who they were. And it hurt her.

He grabbed her wrist. "No argument." He led her outside and down a path to a garden bench, but one of the Grasselle sisters already occupied the space. A man sat on either side and she was flirting for all she was worth.

Alexander sighed. He knew what to do if he wanted privacy. He pulled Merry along until he was at the end of the garden where he pushed open a fence. Then he walked her through a small stretch until they were on the beach. The waves roared around them.

"I know you're in there," he said without preamble. "So don't pretend you aren't."

She turned her head to the right, gazing at nothing.

"This is what we're going to do. Lissa told me that if I married you, you would be happy."

For that she glanced at him. "But you wouldn't be."

"How do you know?" Alexander asked, suddenly feeling he was the one with all the answers for a change. "Lissa promised that I would always know you and in that ballroom when we were dancing, I didn't see a crone. I saw *you*. That means I will always see *you*. Others may see a crone but I will see you. There is no reason for you not to marry me."

She drew a short breath. "You don't love me."

"I'm not exactly sure what difference that makes. The real bottom line is that you will be happy and I will know the truth. Other people may think I'm married to a crone but I'll know I'm not."

"You'll suffer everyone's ridicule."

"I don't care."

Merry scoffed. "Of course you do. Anyone would."

"Not if it means I can bring you some happiness."

To Alexander's surprise her eyes filled with tears again. "That's very sweet, but I won't let you do it."

He stared at her. "Are you insane?"

"No. You don't love me. You've said it a million times. Even if you make me the happiest woman in the world, I won't marry you because then you won't be happy. You don't want to be married. You can't trust. You can't love. I've caused you enough pain, Alexander. I won't cause you any more."

"The pain of seeing you alone and lonely is worse than anything I'd suffer married to you."

"I don't believe that. Goodbye, Alexander."

"Goodbye?" The word sounded so final that panic skittered through him. If Merry left the resort, he couldn't take care of her. "Aren't you staying as Merry Montrose?"

She nodded. "Yes. But it's nearly midnight. After midnight, I probably won't know you as the man I loved. And that's another reason for you not to marry me. If I don't know you, you will get nothing from this relationship."

She began to walk away and Alexander had to raise his voice to be heard above the roar of the waves. "I don't care."

She spun to face him. Her apricot dress fluttered in the breeze. "I do! I would know that you don't love me."

"Dear God, Meredith!" Alexander said; frustration and panic welled up and spilled over. "I'm willing to sacrifice my life for you. How the hell can you say I don't love you?"

Princess Meredith stopped.

Alexander ran his fingers through his hair. The truth of what he had said rattled through him as if taking its rightful place in his life. It grabbed his heart and warned it that pain always accompanied love. It tightened his chest with fear.

But there was no denying it. He loved her. He could not let her live her life alone because he loved her.

"I am willing to sacrifice my life for you because that's what a man does for his betrothed." He paused long enough to catch her hand. "And I believe that proves I love you. You have no more excuses. And if you can take one promise, one piece of knowledge of your old life into your new life, take the promise of my love."

Meredith blinked back tears. "Okay."

"And marry me."

"Okay."

Prince Alec felt his heart stop then speed up to triple time. "Okay?"

Merry squeezed her lips together and nodded. "Yes. Okay."

"Well, dear God, it's about time," Lissa said, pushing her way from between two tall bushes.

Merry gasped, "Lissa!"

Alexander said, "Now what do you want?"

"Now, I'm going to perform the ceremony."

"Right here?" Alexander said, glancing around. The wind was wild as if a storm sat on the horizon waiting to thunder through. The moon had ducked behind the clouds in fear. Waves pounded the shore.

"Oh, I get it. You're here so I don't have a chance to change my mind."

The clock in the hotel tower chimed.

"Exactly," Lissa said as a black book suddenly appeared in her hands. "With the final toll of the bell of that clock, it will be midnight. Merry's birthday. But *you* are Merry's twenty-first love match. When you marry her, the curse is broken."

Merry looked at Alexander and Alexander glanced down at Merry.

"You mean she won't be a crone?"

The clock chimed again. "She will if you don't stop asking questions long enough to say your vows." Lissa flipped through some pages of her black book and finally said, "Let's see . . . Dearly beloved, ya-da-ya-da . . . Do you, Princess Meredith Bessart . . ."

"Lissa!" Merry cried. "You could have given me a minute to explain I was a princess before you used my real name . . ."

". . . take this man to be your lawfully wedded husband?"

She drew a quick breath. "All right. I'll make explanations later. Yes. I do."

"And do you, Prince Alec Montclair . . ."

Merry's mouth fell open. She faced Alexander. "Prince Alec?"

He caught her other hand and drew her closer. "Yes, I, Prince Alec Montclair take this woman to be my lawfully wedded wife. To have and to hold, from this day forward, in sickness and in health, until death do we part."

"Well, thanks for finishing that up." Lissa slammed closed the book. "I now pronounce you husband and wife."

Merry stared at Alexander . . . Prince Alec. Her eyes narrowed with suspicion. He guessed she was probably only now realizing he hadn't protested when Lissa called her a princess and that he might have even known who she was all along.

"You knew."

"Does it matter?"

"Do you really love me?"

"Yes. I love you."

The clock sounded its final chime. The wind off the waves blew up the shore and swirled around them. Sand seemed to suffocate them for several seconds, but in the whirlpool Merry felt her face tightening. The muscles of her arms and legs, back and stomach, hips and chin shifted and strengthened. Even her dress seemed to change. Then just as quickly as the wind arose, it vanished.

When Merry opened her eyes, Prince Alec stood before her in his royal attire. She felt the heaviness of her crown on her head. Glancing down, she saw her favorite gown. A gown that fit all her curves and made her skin look pure and soft. Tears filled her eyes.

"Come along," Lissa said, bossy as ever. "Do you hear the trumpets?"

"Yes."

"You two are about to be announced."

Merry and Prince Alec suddenly stood at the open patio doors of the ballroom. "And

I give you," the bandleader said from the stage, "Prince Alec Montclair and his wife, Princess Meredith Bessart Montclair."

The trumpets sounded but Alexander stopped Merry from entering. "I do love you."

She couldn't help but smile. "The curse wouldn't have been broken if it hadn't been true."

"I needed to say it again."

"And I need to tell you again that I'm sorry for all the hurt I caused you all those years ago."

He put his finger over her lips to silence her. "That was a long time ago." He paused, then smiled. "Those were two different people."

She nodded. "Yes. They were."

"I love you," he said, then kissed her, as his wife, knowing that they would sleep together that night and every night for the rest of their lives. They would have children and the appropriate alliance his country needed. But most of all they would have love. Merry would never be lonely again. And he . . .

Well, he was about to enter into the greatest adventure of all. He was handing his heart to a woman who clearly had enough magic at her disposal to turn him into a frog if she wanted to. . . .

And he wasn't even slightly afraid. He loved her. He trusted her. This was the happiest moment of his life.

About the Author

Susan Meier is one of eleven children, and though she has yet to write a book about a big family, many of her books explore the dynamics of "unusual" family situations, such as large work "families", bosses who behave like overprotective fathers, or "sister" bonds created between friends. Because she has more than twenty nieces and nephews, children also are always popping up in her stories. Many of the funny scenes in her books are based on experiences raising her own children or interacting with her nieces and nephews.

She was born and raised in western Pennsylvania and continues to live in Pennsylvania.

We hope you have enjoyed this Large Print book. Other Thorndike, Wheeler or Chivers Press Large Print books are available at your library or directly from the publishers.

For more information about current and upcoming titles, please call or write, without obligation, to:

Publisher
Thorndike Press
295 Kennedy Memorial Drive
Waterville, ME 04901
Tel. (800) 223-1244

Or visit our Web site at:
www.gale.com/thorndike
www.gale.com/wheeler

OR

Chivers Large Print
published by BBC Audiobooks Ltd
St James House, The Square
Lower Bristol Road
Bath BA2 3SB
England
Tel. +44(0) 800 136919
email: bbcaudiobooks@bbc.co.uk
www.bbcaudiobooks.co.uk

All our Large Print titles are designed for easy reading, and all our books are made to last.